D1091284

THE YALE SHAKESPEARE

EDITED BY

WILBUR L. CROSS TUCKER BROOKE

WILLARD HIGLEY DURHAM

PUBLISHED UNDER THE DIRECTION
OF THE
DEPARTMENT OF ENGLISH, YALE UNIVERSITY,
ON THE FUND
GIVEN TO THE YALE UNIVERSITY PRESS IN 1917
BY THE MEMBERS OF THE
KINGSLEY TRUST ASSOCIATION
TO COMMEMORATE THE SEVENTY-FIFTH ANNIVERSARY
OF THE FOUNDING OF THE SOCIETY

·: *The Yale Shakespeare* :·

THE WINTER'S TALE

EDITED BY

FREDERICK E. PIERCE

NEW HAVEN AND LONDON · YALE UNIVERSITY PRESS

Printed in the United States
of America

TABLE OF CONTENTS

The facsimile opposite reproduces the first page of 'The Winter's Tale' from the earliest printed edition, the Shakespeare Folio of 1623. This play is there the fourteenth in order among the thirty-six in the volume and stands at the end of the division of 'Comedies.' The facsimile has been made from the Elizabethan Club copy of the Folio and is about one-third the size of the original.

The VVinters Tale.

Actus Primus. Scœna Prima.

Enter Camillo and Archidamus.

Arch.

IF you shall chance (*Camillo*) to visit *Bohemia*, on the like occasion whereon my seruices are now on-foot, you shall see (as I haue said) great difference betwixt our *Bohemia*, and your *Sicilia*.

am. I thinke, this comming Summer, the King of *ia* meanes to pay *Bohemia* the Visitation, which hee y owes him.

Arch. Wherein our Entertainment shall shame vs: we be iustified in our Loues: for indeed---

am. 'Beseech you---

Arch. Verely I speake it in the freedome of my know- e: we cannot with such magnificence--- in so rare-- ow not what to say--- Wee will giue you sleepie kes, that your Sences (vn-intelligent of our insuffi- ce) may, though they cannot prayse vs, as little ac- vs.

am. You pay a great deale to deare, for what's giuen y.

Arch. 'Beleeue me, I speake as my vnderstanding in- cts me, and as mine honestie puts it to vtterance.

am. *Sicilia* cannot shew himselfe ouer-kind to *Bohe-* They were trayn'd together in their Child-hoods; there rooted betwixt them then such an affection, ch cannot chuse but braunch now. Since their more ue Dignities, and Royall Necessities, made seperati- f their Societie, their Encounters (though not Perso- hath been Royally attornyed with enter-change of s, Letters, louing Embassies, that they haue seem'd to ogether, though absent: shooke hands, as ouer a Vast; embrac'd as it were from the ends of opposed Winds: Heauens continue their Loues.

rch. I thinke there is not in the World, either Malice Matter, to alter it. You haue an vnspeakable comfort our young Prince *Mamillius*: it is a Gentleman of the test Promise, that euer came into my Note.

am. I very well agree with you, in the hopes of him: a gallant Child; one, that (indeed) Physicks the Sub- makes old hearts fresh: they that went on Crutches e was borne, desire yet their life, to see him a Man.

ch. Would they else be content to die?

m. Yes; if there were no other excuse, why they should e to liue.

Arch. If the King had no Sonne, they would desire to ou Crutches till he had one. *Exeunt.*

Scœna Secunda.

nter Leontes, Hermione, Mamillius, Polixenes, Camillo.

. Nine Changes of the Watry-Starre hath been
The Shepheards Note, since we haue left our Throne
Without a Burthen: Time as long againe
Would be fill'd vp (my Brother) with our Thanks,
And yet we should, for perpetuitie,
Goe hence in debt: And therefore, like a Cypher
(Yet standing in rich place) I multiply
With one we thanke you, many thousands moe,
That goe before it.

Leo. Stay your Thanks a while,
And pay them when you part.

Pol. Sir, that's to morrow:
I am question'd by my feares, of what may chance,
Or breed vpon our absence, that may blow
No sneaping Winds at home, to make vs say,
This is put forth too truly: besides, I haue stay'd
To tyre your Royaltie.

Leo. We are tougher (Brother)
Then you can put vs to't.

Pol. No longer stay.

Leo. One Seue'night longer.

Pol. Very sooth, to morrow.

Leo. Wee'le part the time betweene's then: and in that
Ile no gaine-saying.

Pol. Presse me not ('beseech you) so:
There is no Tongue that moues; none, none i'th' World
So soone as yours, could win me: so it should now,
Were there necessitie in your request, although
'Twere needfull I deny'd it. My Affaires
Doe euen drag me home-ward: which to hinder,
Were (in your Loue) a Whip to me; my stay,
To you a Charge, and Trouble: to saue both,
Farewell (our Brother.)

Leo. Tongue-ty'd our Queene? speake you.

Her. I had thought (Sir) to haue held my peace, vntill
You had drawne Oathes from him, not to stay: you (Sir)
Charge him too coldly. Tell him, you are sure
All in *Bohemia's* well: this satisfaction,
The by-gone-day proclaym'd, say this to him,
He's beat from his best ward.

Leo. Well said, *Hermione.*

Her. To tell, he longs to see his Sonne, were strong:
But let him say so then, and let him goe;
But let him sweare so, and he shall not stay,
Wee'l thwack him hence with Distaffes.
Yet of your Royall presence, Ile aduenture
The borrow of a Weeke. When at *Bohemia*
You take my Lord, Ile giue him my Commission,
To let him there a Moneth, behind the Gest
Prefix'd for's parting: yet (good-deed) *Leontes*,
I loue thee not a Iarre o'th' Clock, behind

[DRAMATIS PERSONÆ]

LEONTES, *King of Sicilia*
MAMILLIUS, *young Prince of Sicilia*
CAMILLO,
ANTIGONUS,
CLEOMENES,
DION,
} *Four Lords of Sicilia*
HERMIONE, *Queen to Leontes*
PERDITA, *Daughter to Leontes and Hermione*
PAULINA, *Wife to Antigonus*
EMILIA, *a Lady*
POLIXENES, *King of Bohemia*
FLORIZEL, *Prince of Bohemia*
Old Shepherd, *reputed Father of Perdita*
Clown, *his Son*
AUTOLYCUS, *a Rogue*
ARCHIDAMUS, *a Lord of Bohemia*
[MOPSA,
[DORCAS,
} *Shepherdesses*]
Other Lords and Gentlemen and Servants
Shepherds and Shepherdesses
[A Mariner
A Gaoler
Ladies attending the Queen
Satyrs for a dance

Time, as Chorus

SCENE: *Sometimes in Sicilia, sometimes in Bohemia.*]

Dramatis Personæ; *cf. n.*

The Winter's Tale

ACT FIRST

Scene One

[*Sicilia. An Antechamber in Leontes' Palace*]

Enter Camillo and Archidamus.

Arch. If you shall chance, Camillo, to visit Bohemia, on the like occasion whereon my services are now on foot, you shall see, as I have said, great difference betwixt our Bohemia and your Sicili.. 5

Cam. I think, this coming summer, the King of Sicilia means to pay Bohemia the visitation which he justly owes him. 8

Arch. Wherein our entertainment shall shame us we will be justified in our loves: for, indeed,—

Cam. Beseech you,— 11

Arch. Verily, I speak it in the freedom of my knowledge: we cannot with such magnificence—in so rare—I know not what to say. We will give you sleepy drinks, that your senses, unintelligent of our insufficience, may, though they cannot praise us, as little accuse us. 17

Cam. You pay a great deal too dear for what 's given freely.

Arch. Believe me, I speak as my understanding instructs me, and as mine honesty puts it to utterance. 22

on foot: *actively employed*
Bohemia: *the king of Bohemia* visitation: *visit*
, 10 entertainment . . . loves; *cf. n.* 11 Beseech: *I beseech*
.2 freedom: *privilege* 15 unintelligent of: *not perceiving*

Cam. Sicilia cannot show himself over-kind to Bohemia. They were trained together in their childhoods; and there rooted betwixt them then such an affection which cannot choose but branch now. Since their more mature dignities and royal necessities made separation of their society, their encounters, though not personal, have been royally attorneyed with interchange of gifts, letters, loving embassies; that they have seemed to be together, though absent, shook hands, as over a vast, and embraced, as it were, from the ends of opposed winds. The heavens continue their loves!

Arch. I think there is not in the world either malice or matter to alter it. You have an unspeakable comfort of your young Prince Mamillius: it is a gentleman of the greatest promise that ever came into my note.

Cam. I very well agree with you in the hopes of him. It is a gallant child; one that indeed physics the subject, makes old hearts fresh; they that went on crutches ere he was born desire yet their life to see him a man.

Arch. Would they else be content to die?

Cam. Yes; if there were no other excuse why they should desire to live.

Arch. If the king had no son, they would desire to live on crutches till he had one.

Exeunt.

23 Sicilia: *the king of Sicily* 26 which: *a*
27 branch: *put forth branches* 29 encounters: *meeting*
30 personal: *performed in person* attorneyed: *performed by proxy*
32 that: *so that* 33 vast: *boundless and waste expanse*
34, 35 from . . . winds; *cf. n.* 40 note: *notice*
43 physics the subject: *is medicine to the king's subjects*

Scene Two

[*A Room of State in the Palace*]

Enter Leontes, Hermione, Mamillius, Polixenes, Camillo, [*and Attendants*].

Pol. Nine changes of the watery star have been
The shepherd's note since we have left our throne
Without a burden: time as long again
Would be fill'd up, my brother, with our thanks;
And yet we should for perpetuity 5
Go hence in debt: and therefore, like a cipher,
Yet standing in rich place, I multiply
With one 'We thank you' many thousands moe
That go before it.
Leon. Stay your thanks awhile, 9
And pay them when you part.
Pol. Sir, that 's to-morrow.
I am question'd by my fears, of what may chance
Or breed upon our absence; that may blow 12
No sneaping winds at home, to make us say,
'This is put forth too truly!' Besides, I have stay'd
To tire your royalty.
Leon. We are tougher, brother,
Than you can put us to 't.
Pol. No longer stay. 16
Leon One seven-night longer.
Pol. Very sooth, to-morrow.
Leon. We'll part the time between 's then; and in that
I'll no gainsaying.

1 watery star: *moon; cf. n.*
2 The shepherd's note: *observed by the shepherd*
6, 7 like . . . place; *cf. n.* 8 moe: *more* 9 Stay: *postpone*
10 part: *depart* 12 that may blow; *cf. n.*
14 is put forth: *has blossomed (resulted)*
16 put us to't: *prove by extreme test*
17 Very sooth: *in absolute truth* 18 between's: *between us*

Pol. Press me not, beseech you, so.
There is no tongue that moves, none, none i' the world, 20
So soon as yours could win me: so it should now,
Were there necessity in your request, although
'Twere needful I denied it. My affairs
Do even drag me homeward; which to hinder 24
Were in your love a whip to me; my stay
To you a charge and trouble: to save both,
Farewell, our brother.

Leon. Tongue-tied, our queen? speak you.

Her. I had thought, sir, to have held my peace until 28
You had drawn oaths from him not to stay. You, sir,
Charge him too coldly: tell him, you are sure
All in Bohemia 's well: this satisfaction
The by-gone day proclaim'd: say this to him, 32
He 's beat from his best ward.

Leon. Well said, Hermione.

Her. To tell he longs to see his son were strong:
But let him say so then, and let him go;
But let him swear so, and he shall not stay, 36
We'll thwack him hence with distaffs.
[*To Polixenes.*] Yet of your royal presence I'll adventure
The borrow of a week. When at Bohemia
You take my lord, I'll give him my commission
To let him there a month behind the gest 41
Prefix'd for 's parting: yet, good deed, Leontes,

25 in your love a whip to me: *an injury to me, though meant in love*
26 charge: *expense* 33 ward: *fencer's guard* 37 thwack: *beat*
38 adventure: *venture* 39 borrow: *borrowing*
40 commission: *permission*
41 let: *allow to remain* gest: *date of departure; cf. n.*
42 good deed: *indeed*

I love thee not a jar o' the clock behind
What lady she her lord. You'll stay?
Pol. No, madam. 44
Her. Nay, but you will?
Pol. I may not, verily.
Her. Verily
You put me off with limber vows; but I,
Though you would seek to unsphere the stars with oaths, 48
Should yet say, 'Sir, no going.' Verily,
You shall not go: a lady's 'verily' 's
As potent as a lord's. Will you go yet?
Force me to keep you as a prisoner, 52
Not like a guest; so you shall pay your fees
When you depart, and save your thanks. How say you?
My prisoner, or my guest? by your dread 'verily,'
One of them you shall be.
Pol. Your guest, then, madam: 56
To be your prisoner should import offending;
Which is for me less easy to commit
Than you to punish.
Her. Not your gaoler then,
But your kind hostess. Come, I'll question you
Of my lord's tricks and yours when you were boys: 61
You were pretty lordings then.
Pol. We were, fair queen,
Two lads that thought there was no more behind
But such a day to-morrow as to-day, 64
And to be boy eternal.
Her. Was not my lord
The verier wag o' the two?

43 jar: *tick*
44 What lady she: *any lady whatever*
47 limber: *easily evaded*
48 unsphere, *etc.; cf. n.*
53 pay your fees; *cf. n.*

Pol. We were as twinn'd lambs that did frisk i' the sun,
And bleat the one at the other: what we chang'd 68
Was innocence for innocence; we knew not
The doctrine of ill-doing, nor dream'd
That any did. Had we pursu'd that life,
And our weak spirits ne'er been higher rear'd 72
With stronger blood, we should have answer'd heaven
Boldly, 'not guilty;' the imposition clear'd
Hereditary ours.

Her. By this we gather
You have tripp'd since.

Pol. O! my most sacred lady, 76
Temptations have since then been born to 's; for
In those unfledg'd days was my wife a girl;
Your precious self had then not cross'd the eyes
Of my young playfellow.

Her. Grace to boot! 80
Of this make no conclusion, lest you say
Your queen and I are devils; yet, go on:
The offences we have made you do we'll answer;
If you first sinn'd with us, and that with us 84
You did continue fault, and that you slipp'd not
With any but with us.

Leon. Is he won yet?

Her. He'll stay, my lord.

Leon. At my request he would not.
Hermione, my dearest, thou never spok'st 88
To better purpose.

Her. Never?

Leon. Never, but once.

68 chang'd: *exchanged* 74 the imposition, *etc.; cf. n.*
80 Grace to boot: *Heavenly Grace help us*

Her. What! have I twice said well? when was 't before?
I prithee tell me; cram 's with praise, and make 's
As fat as tame things: one good deed, dying tongueless, 92
Slaughters a thousand waiting upon that.
Our praises are our wages: you may ride 's
With one soft kiss a thousand furlongs ere
With spur we heat an acre. But to the goal: 96
My last good deed was to entreat his stay:
What was my first? it has an elder sister,
Or I mistake you: O! would her name were Grace.
But once before I spoke to the purpose: when?
Nay, let me have 't; I long.

Leon. Why, that was when
Three crabbed months had sour'd themselves to death,
Ere I could make thee open thy white hand
And clap thyself my love: then didst thou utter, 104
'I am yours for ever.'

Her. 'Tis grace indeed.
Why, lo you now, I have spoke to the purpose twice:
The one for ever earn'd a royal husband,
The other for some while a friend. 108
[*Giving her hand to Polixenes.*]

Leon. [*Aside.*] Too hot, too hot!
To mingle friendship far is mingling bloods.
I have *tremor cordis* on me: my heart dances;
But not for joy; not joy. This entertainment 112
May a free face put on, derive a liberty

92 tame things: *well-fed pets* one good deed, *etc.; cf. n.*
96 heat: *race over* to the goal: *to come to the point*
99 would her name were Grace: *would that that were called a gracious deed!*
104 clap: *declare by clapping thy hand into mine*
111 tremor cordis: *trembling of the heart* 113 free: *innocent*

From heartiness, from bounty, fertile bosom,
And well become the agent: 't may, I grant:
But to be paddling palms and pinching fingers,
As now they are, and making practis'd smiles, 117
As in a looking-glass; and then to sigh, as 'twere
The mort o' the deer; O! that is entertainment
My bosom likes not, nor my brows. Mamillius,
Art thou my boy?

Mam. Ay, my good lord.

Leon. I' fecks? 121
Why, that 's my bawcock. What! hast smutch'd thy nose?
They say it is a copy out of mine. Come, captain,
We must be neat; not neat, but cleanly, captain:
And yet the steer, the heifer, and the calf, 125
Are all call'd neat. Still virginalling
Upon his palm! How now, you wanton calf!
Art thou my calf?

Mam. Yes, if you will, my lord. 128

Leon. Thou want'st a rough pash and the shoots that I have,
To be full like me: yet they say we are
Almost as like as eggs; women say so,
That will say anything: but were they false 132
As o'er-dy'd blacks, as wind, as waters, false
As dice are to be wish'd by one that fixes
No bourn 'twixt his and mine, yet were it true
To say this boy were like me. Come, sir page,

114 fertile: *generous*
119 mort o' the deer: *note on hunter's horn announcing death of the deer*
120 brows; *cf. n.* 121 I' fecks: *in faith*
122 bawcock: *fine lad* smutch'd: *soiled*
126 neat: *cattle* virginalling: *playing with fingers; cf. n.*
129 pash: *head* shoots: *horns*
133 o'er-dy'd blacks: *mourning garments rotten from over-dyeing or worn by hypocritical mourners*
135 bourn: *boundary*

Look on me with your welkin eye: sweet villain!
Most dear'st! my collop! Can thy dam?—may 't
be?—
Affection! thy intention stabs the centre:
Thou dost make possible things not so held, 140
Communicat'st with dreams;—how can this be?—
With what 's unreal thou co-active art,
And fellow'st nothing: then, 'tis very credent
Thou mayst co-join with something; and thou
dost, 144
And that beyond commission, and I find it,
And that to the infection of my brains
And hardening of my brows.

Pol. What means Sicilia?

Her. He something seems unsettled.

Pol. How, my lord! 148

Leon. What cheer? how is 't with you, best
brother?

Her. You look
As if you held a brow of much distraction:
Are you mov'd, my lord?

Leon. No, in good earnest.
How sometimes nature will betray its folly, 152
Its tenderness, and make itself a pastime
To harder bosoms! Looking on the lines
Of my boy's face, methoughts I did recoil
Twenty-three years, and saw myself unbreech'd,
In my green velvet coat, my dagger muzzled,
Lest it should bite its master, and so prove,
As ornaments oft do, too dangerous:
How like, methought, I then was to this kernel,

137 welkin: *sky-blue* villain: *little rogue*
138 my collop: *a piece of my flesh* dam: *mother*
139-144 Affection . . . dost; *cf. n.* 148 something: *somewhat*

This squash, this gentleman. Mine honest friend, 161
Will you take eggs for money?

Mam. No, my lord, I'll fight.

Leon. You will? why, happy man be his dole! My brother,
Are you so fond of your young prince as we 164
Do seem to be of ours?

Pol. If at home, sir,
He 's all my exercise, my mirth, my matter,
Now my sworn friend and then mine enemy;
My parasite, my soldier, statesman, all: 168
He makes a July's day short as December,
And with his varying childness cures in me
Thoughts that would thick my blood.

Leon. So stands this squire
Offic'd with me. We two will walk, my lord, 172
And leave you to your graver steps. Hermione,
How thou lov'st us, show in our brother's welcome:
Let what is dear in Sicily be cheap:
Next to thyself and my young rover, he 's 176
Apparent to my heart.

Her. If you would seek us,
We are yours i' the garden: shall 's attend you there?

Leon. To your own bents dispose you: you'll be found,
Be you beneath the sky.—[*Aside.*] I am angling now, 180
Though you perceive me not how I give line.
Go to, go to!
How she holds up the neb, the bill to him!

161 squash: *an unripe pea-pod*
162 take eggs for money: *allow yourself to be imposed on*
163 dole: *lot in life*
170 childness: *childish humors*
171 thick my blood: *thicken my blood, cause melancholy*
172 Offic'd with: *in relation to*
177 Apparent: *heir apparent*
178 shall's: *shall we*
179 bents: *inclinations*
183 neb: *mouth*

And arms her with the boldness of a wife 184
To her allowing husband!
[*Exeunt Polixenes, Hermione, and Attendants.*]
Gone already!
Inch-thick, knee-deep, o'er head and ears a fork'd one!
Go play, boy, play; thy mother plays, and I
Play too, but so disgrac'd a part, whose issue 188
Will hiss me to my grave: contempt and clamour
Will be my knell. Go play, boy, play. There have been,
Or I am much deceiv'd, cuckolds ere now;
And many a man there is even at this present,
Now, while I speak this, holds his wife by the arm,
That little thinks she has been sluic'd in 's absence,
And his pond fish'd by his next neighbour, by
Sir Smile, his neighbour: nay, there 's comfort in 't, 196
Whiles other men have gates, and those gates open'd,
As mine, against their will. Should all despair
That have revolted wives, the tenth of mankind
Would hang themselves. Physic for 't there is none; 200
It is a bawdy planet, that will strike
Where 'tis predominant; and 'tis powerful, think it,
From east, west, north, and south: be it concluded,
No barricado for a belly: know 't; 204
It will let in and out the enemy
With bag and baggage. Many a thousand on 's
Have the disease, and feel 't not. How now, boy!

Mam. I am like you, they say.

185 allowing: *approving* 186 a fork'd one: *with forked horns*
188 issue: *outcome* 201 strike: *blast*
202 predominant: *strongest in influence; cf. n.*

Leon. Why, that 's some comfort. 208
What! Camillo there?
Cam. Ay, my good lord.
Leon. Go play, Mamillius; thou 'rt an honest man.
[*Exit Mamillius.*]
Camillo, this great sir will yet stay longer. 212
Cam. You had much ado to make his anchor hold:
When you cast out, it still came home.
Leon. Didst note it?
Cam. He would not stay at your petitions; made
His business more material.
Leon. Didst perceive it? 216
[*Aside.*] They're here with me already, whispering, rounding,
'Sicilia is a so-forth.' 'Tis far gone,
When I shall gust it last. How came 't, Camillo,
That he did stay?
Cam. At the good queen's entreaty. 220
Leon. At the queen's, be 't: 'good' should be pertinent;
But so it is, it is not. Was this taken
By any understanding pate but thine?
For thy conceit is soaking; will draw in 224
More than the common blocks: not noted, is 't,
But of the finer natures? by some severals
Of head-piece extraordinary? lower messes
Perchance are to this business purblind? say.
Cam. Business, my lord! I think most understand
Bohemia stays here longer.

214 came home: *came back without catching* 216 material: *important*
217 here with me: *making mocking gestures when mentioning me* rounding: *whispering*
219 gust: *perceive* 222 taken: *understood*
224 conceit: *intelligence* soaking: *capable of absorbing*
225 blocks: *heads* 226 severals: *individuals*
227 lower messes: *men of inferior rank who ate, or messed, at a lower table*

Leon. Ha!
Cam. Stays here longer.
Leon. Ay, but why?
Cam. To satisfy your highness and the entreaties 232
Of our most gracious mistress.
Leon. Satisfy!
The entreaties of your mistress! satisfy!
Let that suffice. I have trusted thee, Camillo,
With all the nearest things to my heart, as well
My chamber-councils, wherein, priest-like, thou
Hast cleans'd my bosom: I from thee departed
Thy penitent reform'd; but we have been
Deceiv'd in thy integrity, deceiv'd 240
In that which seems so.
Cam. Be it forbid, my lord!
Leon. To bide upon 't, thou art not honest; or,
If thou inclin'st that way, thou art a coward,
Which hoxes honesty behind, restraining 244
From course requir'd; or else thou must be counted
A servant grafted in my serious trust,
And therein negligent; or else a fool
That seest a game play'd home, the rich stake drawn, 248
And tak'st it all for jest.
Cam. My gracious lord,
I may be negligent, foolish, and fearful;
In every one of these no man is free,
But that his negligence, his folly, fear, 252
Among the infinite doings of the world,
Sometime puts forth. In your affairs, my lord,

237 chamber-councils: *private affairs* 242 bide: *dwell, lay emphasis*
244 hoxes: *hamstrings*
246 grafted in my serious trust: *whom I have trusted implicitly*
254 puts forth: *reveals itself*

If ever I were wilful-negligent,
It was my folly; if industriously 256
I play'd the fool, it was my negligence,
Not weighing well the end; if ever fearful
To do a thing, where I the issue doubted,
Whereof the execution did cry out 260
Against the non-performance, 'twas a fear
Which oft infects the wisest: these, my lord,
Are such allow'd infirmities that honesty
Is never free of. But, beseech your Grace, 264
Be plainer with me; let me know my trespass
By its own visage; if I then deny it,
'Tis none of mine.

Leon. Ha' not you seen, Camillo,—
But that 's past doubt; you have, or your eye-glass 268
Is thicker than a cuckold's horn,—or heard,—
For to a vision so apparent, rumour
Cannot be mute,—or thought,—for cogitation
Resides not in that man that does not think,—
My wife is slippery? If thou wilt confess,— 273
Or else be impudently negative,
To have nor eyes, nor ears, nor thought,—then say
My wife 's a hobby-horse; deserves a name 276
As rank as any flax-wench that puts to
Before her troth-plight: say 't and justify 't.

Cam. I would not be a stander-by, to hear
My sovereign mistress clouded so, without 280
My present vengeance taken: 'shrew my heart,

260 execution: *successful performance later*
268 eye-glass: *crystalline lens of the eye*
270 vision so apparent: *spectacle so obvious*
273 slippery: *inconstant* 273-275 If . . . thought; *cf. n.*
276 hobby-horse: *immoral woman*
277 flax-wench: *female flax-dresser* puts to: *sins*
280 clouded: *shamefully accused; cf. n.*
281 present: *immediate* 'shrew: *beshrew, curse*

You never spoke what did become you less
Than this; which to reiterate were sin
As deep as that, though true.

Leon. Is whispering nothing? 284
Is leaning cheek to cheek? is meeting noses?
Kissing with inside lip? stopping the career
Of laughter with a sigh?—a note infallible
Of breaking honesty,—horsing foot on foot? 288
Skulking in corners? wishing clocks more swift?
Hours, minutes? noon, midnight? and all eyes
Blind with the pin and web but theirs, theirs only,
That would unseen be wicked? is this nothing?
Why, then the world and all that 's in 't is nothing; 293
The covering sky is nothing; Bohemia nothing;
My wife is nothing; nor nothing have these nothings,
If this be nothing.

Cam. Good my lord, be cur'd 296
Of this diseas'd opinion, and betimes;
For 'tis most dangerous.

Leon. Say it be, 'tis true.

Cam. No, no, my lord.

Leon. It is; you lie, you lie:
I say thou liest, Camillo, and I hate thee; 300
Pronounce thee a gross lout, a mindless slave,
Or else a hovering temporizer, that
Canst with thine eyes at once see good and evil,
Inclining to them both: were my wife's liver 304
Infected as her life, she would not live
The running of one glass.

Cam. Who does infect her?

288 honesty: *chastity* 291 pin and web: *cataract*
306 glass: *hour-glass*

Leon. Why, he that wears her like her medal, hanging
About his neck, Bohemia: who, if I 308
Had servants true about me, that bare eyes
To see alike mine honour as their profits,
Their own particular thrifts, they would do that
Which should undo more doing: ay, and thou,
His cup-bearer,—whom I from meaner form 313
Have bench'd and rear'd to worship, who mayst see
Plainly, as heaven sees earth, and earth sees heaven,
How I am galled,—mightst bespice a cup, 316
To give mine enemy a lasting wink;
Which draught to me were cordial.

Cam. Sir, my lord,
I could do this, and that with no rash potion,
But with a lingering dram that should not work
Maliciously like poison: but I cannot 321
Believe this crack to be in my dread mistress,
So sovereignly being honourable.
I have lov'd thee,—

Leon. Make that thy question, and go rot!
Dost think I am so muddy, so unsettled, 325
To appoint myself in this vexation; sully
The purity and whiteness of my sheets,
Which to preserve is sleep; which being spotted
Is goads, thorns, nettles, tails of wasps? 329
Give scandal to the blood o' the prince my son,
Who I do think is mine, and love as mine,
Without ripe moving to 't? Would I do this?

307 medal; *cf. n.* 311 thrifts: *advantages*
313 meaner form: *lower seat*
314 bench'd: *given a seat of authority* worship: *dignity, honor*
316 bespice: *poison* 317 wink: *sleep* 319 rash: *speedy*
321 Maliciously: *violently* 322 crack: *flaw*
323 sovereignly: *above all others* 324 question: *subject for thought*
326 appoint: *dress* 332 ripe moving to 't: *ample cause for it*

Could man so blench?

Cam. I must believe you, sir: 333

I do; and will fetch off Bohemia for 't;
Provided that when he 's remov'd, your highness
Will take again your queen as yours at first, 336
Even for your son's sake; and thereby for sealing
The injury of tongues in courts and kingdoms
Known and allied to yours.

Leon. Thou dost advise me

Even so as I mine own course have set down:
I'll give no blemish to her honour, none. 341

Cam. My lord,

Go then; and with a countenance as clear
As friendship wears at feasts, keep with Bohemia,
And with your queen. I am his cupbearer; 345
If from me he have wholesome beverage,
Account me not your servant.

Leon. This is all:

Do 't, and thou hast the one half of my heart;
Do 't not, thou split'st thine own.

Cam. I'll do 't, my lord. 349

Leon. I will seem friendly, as thou hast advis'd me.

Exit.

Cam. O miserable lady! But, for me,

What case stand I in? I must be the poisoner
Of good Polixenes; and my ground to do 't 353
Is the obedience to a master; one
Who, in rebellion with himself, will have
All that are his so too. To do this deed 356
Promotion follows. If I could find example
Of thousands that had struck anointed kings,

333 blench: *start aside from his course*
334 fetch off: *make away with* 337 sealing: *sealing up, ending*
338 injury of tongues: *injury caused by gossip*

And flourish'd after, I'd not do 't; but since
Nor brass nor stone nor parchment bears not one, 360
Let villainy itself forswear 't. I must
Forsake the court: to do 't, or no, is certain
To me a break-neck. Happy star reign now!
Here comes Bohemia.

Enter Polixenes.

Pol. This is strange: methinks 364
My favour here begins to warp. Not speak?—
Good day, Camillo.

Cam. Hail, most royal sir!

Pol. What is the news i' the court?

Cam. None rare, my lord.

Pol. The king hath on him such a countenance 368
As he had lost some province and a region
Lov'd as he loves himself: even now I met him
With customary compliment, when he,
Wafting his eyes to the contrary, and falling 372
A lip of much contempt, speeds from me and
So leaves me to consider what is breeding
That changes thus his manners.

Cam. I dare not know, my lord. 376

Pol. How! dare not! do not! Do you know, and dare not
Be intelligent to me? 'Tis thereabouts;
For, to yourself, what you do know, you must,
And cannot say you dare not. Good Camillo,
Your chang'd complexions are to me a mirror
Which shows me mine chang'd too; for I must be
A party in this alteration, finding
Myself thus alter'd with 't.

363 break-neck: *ruinous course*
372 contrary: *opposite direction* falling: *letting fall*
378 intelligent: *communicative* thereabouts: *about that*

Cam. There is a sickness 384
Which puts some of us in distemper; but
I cannot name the disease, and it is caught
Of you that yet are well.
Pol. How! caught of me?
Make me not sighted like the basilisk: 388
I have look'd on thousands, who have sped the better
By my regard, but kill'd none so. Camillo,—
As you are certainly a gentleman, thereto
Clerk-like experienc'd, which no less adorns 392
Our gentry than our parents' noble names,
In whose success we are gentle,—I beseech you,
If you know aught which does behove my knowledge
Thereof to be inform'd, imprison it not 396
In ignorant concealment.
Cam. I may not answer.
Pol. A sickness caught of me, and yet I well!
I must be answer'd. Dost thou hear, Camillo;
I conjure thee, by all the parts of man 400
Which honour does acknowledge,—whereof the least
Is not this suit of mine,—that thou declare
What incidency thou dost guess of harm
Is creeping toward me; how far off, how near;
Which way to be prevented if to be; 405
If not, how best to bear it.
Cam. Sir, I will tell you;
Since I am charg'd in honour and by him
That I think honourable. Therefore mark my counsel, 408

388 Make me not sighted: *do not represent me as having eyes* basilisk: *fabulous monster whose glance was fatal*
389 sped: *fared* 390 regard: *look* 391 thereto: *in addition*
392 Clerk-like: *like a scholar* 393 gentry: *noble birth*
394 In whose success: *in succession or descent from whom* gentle: *of high rank*
397 ignorant: *causing ignorance*
400 parts: *traits and qualities* 403 incidency: *happening*

Which must be even as swiftly follow'd as
I mean to utter it, or both yourself and me
Cry 'lost,' and so good night!

Pol. On, good Camillo.

Cam. I am appointed him to murder you. 412

Pol. By whom, Camillo?

Cam. By the king.

Pol. For what?

Cam. He thinks, nay, with all confidence he swears,
As he had seen 't or been an instrument
To vice you to 't, that you have touch'd his queen
Forbiddenly.

Pol. O, then my best blood turn 417
To an infected jelly, and my name
Be yok'd with his that did betray the Best!
Turn then my freshest reputation to 420
A savour, that may strike the dullest nostril
Where I arrive; and my approach be shunn'd,
Nay, hated too, worse than the great'st infection
That e'er was heard or read!

Cam. Swear his thought over
By each particular star in heaven and 425
By all their influences, you may as well
Forbid the sea for to obey the moon
As or by oath remove or counsel shake 428
The fabric of his folly, whose foundation
Is pil'd upon his faith, and will continue
The standing of his body.

Pol. How should this grow?

Cam. I know not: but I am sure 'tis safer to
Avoid what 's grown than question how 'tis born.
If therefore you dare trust my honesty,

412 him: *the one* 416 vice: *force*
424 Swear his thought over: *try to overcome his suspicion by oaths*
428 or . . . or: *either . . . or* 430 continue: *last as long as*

That lies enclosed in this trunk, which you
Shall bear along impawn'd, away to-night! 436
Your followers I will whisper to the business,
And will by twos and threes at several posterns
Clear them o' the city. For myself, I'll put
My fortunes to your service, which are here 440
By this discovery lost. Be not uncertain;
For, by the honour of my parents, I
Have utter'd truth, which, if you seek to prove,
I dare not stand by; nor shall you be safer 444
Than one condemn'd by the king's own mouth, thereon
His execution sworn.

Pol. I do believe thee:
I saw his heart in 's face. Give me thy hand:
Be pilot to me and thy places shall 448
Still neighbour mine. My ships are ready and
My people did expect my hence departure
Two days ago. This jealousy
Is for a precious creature: as she 's rare 452
Must it be great, and, as his person 's mighty
Must it be violent, and, as he does conceive
He is dishonour'd by a man which ever
Profess'd to him, why, his revenges must 456
In that be made more bitter. Fear o'ershades me:
Good expedition be my friend, and comfort
The gracious queen, part of his theme, but nothing
Of his ill-ta'en suspicion! Come, Camillo; 460
I will respect thee as a father if
Thou bear'st my life off hence: let us avoid.

435 trunk: *body* 436 impawn'd: *as a pledge*
438 posterns: *small gates in city walls*
439 Clear them o': *get them away from*
441 discovery: *revelation* uncertain: *undecided*
448 places: *official positions* 456 Profess'd: *professed friendship*
458-460 *Cf. n.* 462 avoid: *depart*

Cam. It is in mine authority to command
The keys of all the posterns: please your highness 464
To take the urgent hour. Come, sir, away!
Exeunt.

ACT SECOND

Scene One

[*A Room in the Palace*]

Enter Hermione, Mamillius, and Ladies.

Her. Take the boy to you: he so troubles me,
'Tis past enduring.
First Lady. Come, my gracious lord,
Shall I be your playfellow?
Mam. No, I'll none of you.
First Lady. Why, my sweet lord? 4
Mam. You'll kiss me hard and speak to me as if
I were a baby still. I love you better.
Sec. Lady. And why so, my lord?
Mam. Not for because
Your brows are blacker; yet black brows, they say, 8
Become some women best, so that there be not
Too much hair there, but in a semicircle,
Or a half-moon made with a pen.
Sec. Lady. Who taught you this?
Mam. I learn'd it out of women's faces. Pray now, 12
What colour are your eyebrows?
First Lady. Blue, my lord.
Mam. Nay, that's a mock: I have seen a lady's nose

Scene One S. d.; *cf. n.* 9 so that: *provided that*

That has been blue, but not her eyebrows.
Sec. Lady. Hark ye;
The queen your mother rounds apace: we shall
Present our services to a fine new prince 17
One of these days; and then you 'd wanton with us,
If we would have you.
First Lady. She is spread of late
Into a goodly bulk: good time encounter her! 20
Her. What wisdom stirs amongst you? Come, sir, now
I am for you again: pray you, sit by us,
And tell 's a tale.
Mam. Merry or sad shall 't be?
Her. As merry as you will.
Mam. A sad tale 's best for winter. 24
I have one of sprites and goblins.
Her. Let 's have that, good sir.
Come on, sit down: come on, and do your best
To fright me with your sprites; you're powerful at it.
Mam. There was a man,—
Her. Nay, come, sit down; then on. 28
Mam. Dwelt by a churchyard. I will tell it softly;
Yond crickets shall not hear it.
Her. Come on then,
And give 't me in mine ear.

[*Enter Leontes, Antigonus, Lords, and Others.*]

Leon. Was he met there? his train? Camillo with him? 32
First Lord. Behind the tuft of pines I met them: never
Saw I men scour so on their way: I ey'd them
Even to their ships.

18 wanton: *play* 22 for you: *at your service* 34 scour: *hasten*

Leon. How blest am I
In my just censure, in my true opinion! 36
Alack, for lesser knowledge! How accurs'd
In being so blest! There may be in the cup
A spider steep'd, and one may drink, depart,
And yet partake no venom, for his knowledge 40
Is not infected; but if one present
The abhorr'd ingredient to his eye, make known
How he hath drunk, he cracks his gorge, his sides,
With violent hefts. I have drunk, and seen the
spider. 44
Camillo was his help in this, his pandar:
There is a plot against my life, my crown;
All 's true that is mistrusted: that false villain
Whom I employ'd was pre-employ'd by him: 48
He has discover'd my design, and I
Remain a pinch'd thing; yea, a very trick
For them to play at will. How came the posterns
So easily open?

First Lord. By his great authority; 52
Which often hath no less prevail'd than so
On your command.

Leon. I know 't too well.
[*To Hermione.*] Give me the boy: I am glad you did
not nurse him:
Though he does bear some signs of me, yet you
Have too much blood in him.

Her. What is this? sport?

Leon. Bear the boy hence; he shall not come about
her;

36 censure: *judgment*
37 Alack, for lesser knowledge: *would I had known less!*
40 partake no venom; *cf. n.* 43 gorge: *throat* 44 hefts: *retchings*
49 discover'd: *revealed* 50 pinch'd: *ridiculous* trick: *trifle, toy*

Away with him!— [*Exit Mamillius, attended.*]
and let her sport herself
With that she 's big with; for 'tis Polixenes 60
Has made thee swell thus.

Her. But I'd say he had not,
And I'll be sworn you would believe my saying,
Howe'er you lean to the nayward.

Leon. You, my lords,
Look on her, mark her well; be but about 64
To say, 'she is a goodly lady,' and
The justice of your hearts will thereto add,
''Tis pity she 's not honest, honourable:'
Praise her but for this her without-door form,—
Which, on my faith deserves high speech,—and straight 69
The shrug, the hum or ha, these petty brands
That calumny doth use,—O, I am out!—
That mercy does, for calumny will sear 72
Virtue itself: these shrugs, these hums and ha's,
When you have said 'she 's goodly,' come between,
Ere you can say 'she 's honest.' But be 't known,
From him that has most cause to grieve it should be, 76
She 's an adulteress.

Her. Should a villain say so,
The most replenish'd villain in the world,
He were as much more villain: you, my lord,
Do but mistake.

Leon. You have mistook, my lady, 80
Polixenes for Leontes. O thou thing!
Which I'll not call a creature of thy place,

63 nayward: *contrary* 67 honest: *chaste*
68 without-door form: *external appearance*
71 out: *wrong, like an actor who has forgotten his part*
78 replenish'd: *complete* 82 place: *high rank*

Lest barbarism, making me the precedent,
Should a like language use to all degrees, 84
And mannerly distinguishment leave out
Betwixt the prince and beggar: I have said
She 's an adulteress; I have said with whom:
More, she 's a traitor, and Camillo is 88
A federary with her, and one that knows
What she should shame to know herself
But with her most vile principal, that she 's
A bed-swerver, even as bad as those 92
That vulgars give bold'st titles; ay, and privy
To this their late escape.

Her. No, by my life,
Privy to none of this. How will this grieve you
When you shall come to clearer knowledge that
You thus have publish'd me! Gentle my lord, 97
You scarce can right me throughly then to say
You did mistake.

Leon. No; if I mistake
In those foundations which I build upon, 100
The centre is not big enough to bear
A schoolboy's top. Away with her to prison!
He who shall speak for her is afar off guilty
But that he speaks.

Her. There 's some ill planet reigns: 104
I must be patient till the heavens look
With an aspect more favourable. Good my lords,
I am not prone to weeping, as our sex
Commonly are; the want of which vain dew 108
Perchance shall dry your pities; but I have

89 federary: *confederate, accomplice* 91 principal: *leader in sin*
92 bed-swerver: *adulteress* 93 vulgars: *the vulgar*
97 publish'd: *denounced publicly* 98 throughly: *thoroughly*
101 centre: *earth* 103 afar off: *indirectly*
106 aspect: *position and influence of a planet*

That honourable grief lodg'd here which burns
Worse than tears drown. Beseech you all, my lords,
With thoughts so qualified as your charities 112
Shall best instruct you, measure me; and so
The king's will be perform'd!

Leon. [*To the Guards.*] Shall I be heard?

Her. Who is 't that goes with me? Beseech your highness,
My women may be with me; for you see 116
My plight requires it. Do not weep, good fools;
There is no cause: when you shall know your mistres
Has deserv'd prison, then abound in tears
As I come out: this action I now go on 120
Is for my better grace. Adieu, my lord:
I never wish'd to see you sorry; now
I trust I shall. My women, come; you have leave.

Leon. Go, do our bidding: hence! 124

[*Exeunt Queen guarded, and Ladies.*]

First Lord. Beseech your highness call the queen again.

Ant. Be certain what you do, sir, lest your justice
Prove violence: in the which three great ones suffer,
Yourself, your queen, your son.

First Lord. For her, my lord, 128
I dare my life lay down, and will do 't, sir,
Please you to accept it,—that the queen is spotless
I' the eyes of heaven and to you: I mean,
In this which you accuse her.

Ant. If it prove 132
She 's otherwise, I'll keep my stables where
I lodge my wife; I'll go in couples with her;

112 qualified: *moderated* 113 measure: *judge*
117 fools: *a term of endearment, not contempt*
120 action: *legal accusation*
130 Please you: *if you please* 133, 134 I'll . . . wife; *cf. n.*

Than when I feel and see her no further trust her;
For every inch of woman in the world, 136
Ay, every dram of woman's flesh is false,
If she be.

Leon. Hold your peaces!

First Lord. Good my lord,—

Ant. It is for you we speak, not for ourselves.
You are abus'd, and by some putter-on 140
That will be damn'd for 't; would I knew the villain,
I would land-damn him. Be she honour-flaw'd,—
I have three daughters; the eldest is eleven,
The second and the third, nine and some five; 144
If this prove true, they'll pay for 't: by mine honour,
I'll geld them all; fourteen they shall not see,
To bring false generations: they are co-heirs;
And I had rather glib myself than they 148
Should not produce fair issue.

Leon. Cease! no more.
You smell this business with a sense as cold
As is a dead man's nose; but I do see 't and feel 't,
As you feel doing thus, and see withal 152
The instruments that feel.

Ant. If it be so,
We need no grave to bury honesty:
There 's not a grain of it the face to sweeten
Of the whole dungy earth.

Leon. What! lack I credit? 156

First Lord. I had rather you did lack than I, my lord,
Upon this ground; and more it would content me
To have her honour true than your suspicion,

140 abus'd: *deceived* putter-on: *instigator, plotter*
142 land-damn; *cf. n.* 147 co-heirs: *equal heirs in default of sons*
148 glib: *geld* 152 *Cf. n.*

Be blam'd for 't how you might.
Leon. Why, what need we 160
Commune with you of this, but rather follow
Our forceful instigation? Our prerogative
Calls not your counsels, but our natural goodness
Imparts this; which if you,—or stupefied 164
Or seeming so in skill,—cannot or will not
Relish a truth like us, inform yourselves
We need no more of your advice: the matter,
The loss, the gain, the ordering on 't, is all 168
Properly ours.
Ant. And I wish, my liege,
You had only in your silent judgment tried it,
Without more overture.
Leon. How could that be?
Either thou art most ignorant by age, 172
Or thou wert born a fool. Camillo's flight,
Added to their familiarity,
Which was as gross as ever touch'd conjecture,
That lack'd sight only, nought for approbation
But only seeing, all other circumstances 177
Made up to the deed, doth push on this proceeding:
Yet, for a greater confirmation,—
For in an act of this importance 'twere 180
Most piteous to be wild,—I have dispatch'd in post
To sacred Delphos, to Apollo's temple,
Cleomenes and Dion, whom you know
Of stuff'd sufficiency. Now, from the oracle 184
They will bring all; whose spiritual counsel had,
Shall stop or spur me. Have I done well?
First Lord. Well done, my lord.

162 forceful instigation: *strong impulse or incitement*
166 Relish: *appreciate*
171 overture: *disclosure*
175-178 Which . . . deed; *cf. n.*
181 wild: *hasty* post: *haste*
182 Delphos; *cf. n.*
184 stuff'd sufficiency: *ample ability*

Leon. Though I am satisfied and need no more 188
Than what I know, yet shall the oracle
Give rest to the minds of others, such as he
Whose ignorant credulity will not
Come up to the truth. So have we thought it good 192
From our free person she should be confin'd,
Lest that the treachery of the two fled hence
Be left her to perform. Come, follow us:
We are to speak in public; for this business 196
Will raise us all.

Ant. [*Aside.*] To laughter, as I take it,
If the good truth were known. *Exeunt.*

Scene Two

[*At the Gate of a Prison*]

Enter Paulina [*and Attendants*].

Paul. The keeper of the prison, call to him;
Let him have knowledge who I am.—[*Exit an Attendant.*] Good lady,
No court in Europe is too good for thee;
What dost thou then in prison?

[*Enter Attendant with the Gaoler.*]

Now, good sir, 4
You know me, do you not?

Gaol. For a worthy lady
And one whom much I honour.

Paul. Pray you then,
Conduct me to the queen.

Gaol. I may not, madam: to the contrary 8
I have express commandment.

193 free: *accessible to everybody*

Paul. Here 's ado,
To lock up honesty and honour from
The access of gentle visitors! Is 't lawful, pray you,
To see her women? any of them? Emilia? 12

Gaol. So please you, madam,
To put apart these your attendants, I
Shall bring Emilia forth.

Paul. I pray now, call her.
Withdraw yourselves. [*Exeunt Attendants.*]

Gaol. And, madam, 16
I must be present at your conference.

Paul. Well, be 't so, prithee. [*Exit Gaoler.*]
Here 's such ado to make no stain a stain
As passes colouring.

[*Enter Gaoler, with Emilia.*]

Dear gentlewoman, 20
How fares our gracious lady?

Emil. As well as one so great and so forlorn
May hold together. On her frights and griefs,—
Which never tender lady hath borne greater,—
She is something before her time deliver'd. 25

Paul. A boy?

Emil. A daughter; and a goodly babe,
Lusty and like to live: the queen receives
Much comfort in 't; says, 'My poor prisoner, 28
I am innocent as you.'

Paul. I dare be sworn:
These dangerous unsafe lunes i' the king, beshrew them!
He must be told on 't, and he shall: the office
Becomes a woman best; I'll take 't upon me. 32

20 colouring: *glossing over* 27 like: *likely*
30 lunes: *lunatic freaks* beshrew: *curse*

If I prove honey-mouth'd, let my tongue blister,
And never to my red-look'd anger be
The trumpet any more. Pray you, Emilia,
Commend my best obedience to the queen: 36
If she dares trust me with her little babe,
I'll show it to the king and undertake to be
Her advocate to the loud'st. We do not know
How he may soften at the sight of the child: 40
The silence often of pure innocence
Persuades when speaking fails.

Emil. Most worthy madam,
Your honour and your goodness is so evident
That your free undertaking cannot miss 44
A thriving issue: there is no lady living
So meet for this great errand. Please your ladyship
To visit the next room, I'll presently
Acquaint the queen of your most noble offer, 48
Who but to-day hammer'd of this design,
But durst not tempt a minister of honour,
Lest she should be denied.

Paul. Tell her, Emilia,
I'll use that tongue I have: if wit flow from 't 52
As boldness from my bosom, let it not be doubted
I shall do good.

Emil. Now be you blest for it!
I'll to the queen. Please you, come something nearer.

Gaol. Madam, if 't please the queen to send the babe, 56
I know not what I shall incur to pass it,
Having no warrant.

Paul. You need not fear it, sir:

44 free: *magnanimous* 45 thriving issue: *successful result*
46 meet: *well fitted* 47 presently: *instantly*
49 hammer'd of: *thought over* 50 minister: *agent* 52 wit: *wisdom*

The child was prisoner to the womb, and is
By law and process of great nature thence 60
Freed and enfranchis'd; not a party to
The anger of the king, nor guilty of,
If any be, the trespass of the queen.
Gaol. I do believe it. 64
Paul. Do not you fear: upon mine honour, I
Will stand betwixt you and danger. *Exeunt.*

Scene Three

[*A Room in the Palace*]

Enter Leontes, Servants, Antigonus, and Lords.

Leon. Nor night, nor day, no rest; it is but weakness
To bear the matter thus; mere weakness. If
The cause were not in being,—part o' the cause,
She the adultress; for the harlot king 4
Is quite beyond mine arm, out of the blank
And level of my brain, plot-proof; but she
I can hook to me: say, that she were gone,
Given to the fire, a moiety of my rest 8
Might come to me again. Who 's there?
First Atten. [*Advancing.*] My lord?
Leon. How does the boy?
First Atten. He took good rest to-night;
'Tis hop'd his sickness is discharg'd.
Leon. To see his nobleness! 12
Conceiving the dishonour of his mother,
He straight declin'd, droop'd, took it deeply,
Fasten'd and fix'd the shame on 't in himself,
Threw off his spirit, his appetite, his sleep, 16

5 blank: *white spot in the middle of target* 6 level: *aim*
8 moiety: *part, usually half* 15 on: *of*

And downright languish'd. Leave me solely: go,
See how he fares. [*Exit Attendant.*]
Fie, fie! no thought of him;
The very thought of my revenges that way
Recoil upon me: in himself too mighty, 20
And in his parties, his alliance; let him be
Until a time may serve: for present vengeance,
Take it on her. Camillo and Polixenes
Laugh at me; make their pastime at my sorrow: 24
They should not laugh, if I could reach them, nor
Shall she within my power.

Enter Paulina [*with a Child*].

First Lord. You must not enter.

Paul. Nay, rather, good my lords, be second to me:
Fear you his tyrannous passion more, alas, 28
Than the queen's life? a gracious innocent soul,
More free than he is jealous.

Ant. That's enough.

Sec. Atten. Madam, he hath not slept to-night; commanded
None should come at him.

Paul. Not so hot, good sir; 32
I come to bring him sleep. 'Tis such as you,
That creep like shadows by him and do sigh
At each his needless heavings, such as you
Nourish the cause of his awaking: I 36
Do come with words as med'cinal as true,
Honest as either, to purge him of that humour
That presses him from sleep.

Leon. What noise there, ho?

17 solely: *alone* 27 second: *lending support*
35 each: *each of* heavings: *sighings* 38 humour; *cf. n.*

Paul. No noise, my lord; but needful confer-
ence 40
About some gossips for your highness.
Leon. How!
Away with that audacious lady! Antigonus,
I charg'd thee that she should not come about me:
I knew she would.
Ant. I told her so, my lord, 44
On your displeasure's peril, and on mine,
She should not visit you.
Leon. What! canst not rule her?
Paul. From all dishonesty he can: in this,
Unless he take the course that you have done,
Commit me for committing honour, trust it, 49
He shall not rule me.
Ant. La you now! you hear;
When she will take the rein I let her run;
But she'll not stumble.
Paul. Good my liege, I come, 52
And I beseech you, hear me, who professes
Myself your loyal servant, your physician,
Your most obedient counsellor, yet that dares
Less appear so in comforting your evils 56
Than such as most seem yours: I say, I come
From your good queen.
Leon. Good queen!
Paul. Good queen, my lord, good queen; I say,
good queen;
And would by combat make her good, so were I
A man, the worst about you.
Leon. Force her hence. 61

41 gossips: *godparents for the child*
49 Commit . . . committing: *imprison . . . putting in practice*
56 comforting your evils: *encouraging your evil acts*

Paul. Let him that makes but trifles of his eyes
First hand me: on mine own accord I'll off;
But first I'll do my errand. The good queen, 64
For she is good, hath brought you forth a daughter:
Here 'tis; commends it to your blessing.
[*Laying down the Child.*]

Leon. Out!
A mankind witch! Hence with her, out o' door:
A most intelligencing bawd!

Paul. Not so; 68
I am as ignorant in that as you
In so entitling me, and no less honest
Than you are mad; which is enough, I'll warrant,
As this world goes, to pass for honest.

Leon. Traitors! 72
Will you not push her out? Give her the bastard.
[*To Antigonus.*] Thou dotard! thou art woman-tir'd, unroosted
By thy dame Partlet here. Take up the bastard;
Take 't up, I say; give 't to thy crone.

Paul. For ever 76
Unvenerable be thy hands, if thou
Tak'st up the princess by that forced baseness
Which he has put upon 't!

Leon. He dreads his wife.

Paul. So I would you did; then, 'twere past all doubt, 80
You'd call your children yours.

Leon. A nest of traitors!

Ant. I am none, by this good light.

Paul. Nor I; nor any

63 hand: *lay hands on* 67 mankind: *mannish*
68 intelligencing: *acting as go-between* 74 woman-tir'd: *hen-pecked*
75 dame Partlet: *lecturing wife; cf. n.*
78 forced baseness: *arbitrarily imposed title of bastard*

But one that 's here, and that 's himself; for he
The sacred honour of himself, his queen's, 84
His hopeful son's, his babe's, betrays to slander,
Whose sting is sharper than the sword's; and will
not,—
For, as the case now stands, it is a curse
He cannot be compell'd to 't,—once remove 88
The root of his opinion, which is rotten
As ever oak or stone was sound.

Leon. A callat
Of boundless tongue, who late hath beat her husband
And now baits me! This brat is none of mine;
It is the issue of Polixenes: 93
Hence with it; and, together with the dam
Commit them to the fire!

Paul. It is yours;
And, might we lay the old proverb to your charge, 96
'So like you, 'tis the worse.' Behold, my lords,
Although the print be little, the whole matter
And copy of the father; eye, nose, lip,
The trick of 's frown, his forehead, nay, the
valley, 100
The pretty dimples of his chin and cheek, his smiles,
The very mould and frame of hand, nail, finger:
And thou, good goddess Nature, which hast made it
So like to him that got it, if thou hast 104
The ordering of the mind too, 'mongst all colours
No yellow in 't; lest she suspect, as he does,
Her children not her husband's.

Leon. A gross hag!
And, lozel, thou art worthy to be hang'd, 108
That wilt not stay her tongue.

90 callat: *disreputable woman* 104 got: *begot*
106 yellow: *the color symbolizing jealousy* 108 lozel: *worthless rascal*

Ant. Hang all the husbands
That cannot do that feat, you'll leave yourself
Hardly one subject.

Leon. Once more, take her hence.

Paul. A most unworthy and unnatural lord
Can do no more.

Leon. I'll ha' thee burn'd.

Paul. I care not:
It is a heretic that makes the fire,
Not she which burns in 't. I'll not call you tyrant;
But this most cruel usage of your queen,— 116
Not able to produce more accusation
Than your own weak-hing'd fancy,—something savours
Of tyranny, and will ignoble make you,
Yea, scandalous to the world.

Leon. On your allegiance, 120
Out of the chamber with her! Were I a tyrant,
Where were her life? she durst not call me so
If she did know me one. Away with her!

Paul. I pray you do not push me; I'll be gone. 124
Look to your babe, my lord; 'tis yours: Jove send her
A better guiding spirit! What need these hands?
You, that are thus so tender o'er his follies,
Will never do him good, not one of you. 128
So, so: farewell; we are gone. *Exit.*

Leon. Thou, traitor, hast set on thy wife to this.
My child! away with 't!—even thou, that hast
A heart so tender o'er it, take it hence 132
And see it instantly consum'd with fire:
Even thou and none but thou. Take it up straight:
Within this hour bring me word 'tis done,—
And by good testimony,—or I'll seize thy life,
With what thou else call'st thine. If thou refuse

And wilt encounter with my wrath, say so;
The bastard brains with these my proper hands
Shall I dash out. Go, take it to the fire; 140
For thou sett'st on thy wife.

Ant. I did not, sir:
These lords, my noble fellows, if they please,
Can clear me in 't.

First Lord. We can, my royal liege,
He is not guilty of her coming hither. 144

Leon. You are liars all.

First Lord. Beseech your highness, give us better credit:
We have always truly serv'd you, and beseech you
So to esteem of us; and on our knees we beg, 148
As recompense of our dear services
Past and to come, that you do change this purpose,
Which being so horrible, so bloody, must
Lead on to some foul issue. We all kneel. 152

Leon. I am a feather for each wind that blows.
Shall I live on to see this bastard kneel
And call me father? Better burn it now
Than curse it then. But, be it; let it live: 156
It shall not neither.—[*To Antigonus.*] You, sir, come you hither;
You that have been so tenderly officious
With Lady Margery, your midwife there,
To save this bastard's life,—for 'tis a bastard, 160
So sure as this beard's grey,—what will you adventure
To save this brat's life?

Ant. Anything, my lord,
That my ability may undergo,

139 proper: *own* 142 fellows: *comrades* 149 dear: *loving*
159 Lady Margery: *a contemptuous term* 161 this: *Antigonus'*

And nobleness impose: at least, thus much: 164
I'll pawn the little blood which I have left,
To save the innocent: anything possible.

Leon. It shall be possible. Swear by this sword
Thou wilt perform my bidding.

Ant. I will, my lord. 168

Leon. Mark and perform it,—seest thou!—for the fail
Of any point in 't shall not only be
Death to thyself, but to thy lewd-tongu'd wife,
Whom for this time we pardon. We enjoin thee,
As thou art liegeman to us, that thou carry 173
This female bastard hence; and that thou bear it
To some remote and desert place quite out
Of our dominions; and that there thou leave it,
Without more mercy, to it own protection, 177
And favour of the climate. As by strange fortune
It came to us, I do in justice charge thee,
On thy soul's peril and thy body's torture, 180
That thou commend it strangely to some place,
Where chance may nurse or end it. Take it up.

Ant. I swear to do this, though a present death
Had been more merciful. Come on, poor babe:
Some powerful spirit instruct the kites and ravens 185
To be thy nurses! Wolves and bears, they say,
Casting their savageness aside have done
Like offices of pity. Sir, be prosperous 188
In more than this deed does require! And blessing
Against this cruelty fight on thy side,
Poor thing, condemn'd to loss!

Exit [*with the Child*].

169 fail: *failure* 177 it: *its*
181 commend: *entrust* strangely: *as a stranger*
189 require: *deserve* 191 loss: *being abandoned*

Leon. No; I'll not rear
Another's issue.

Enter a Servant.

Serv. Please your highness, posts 192
From those you sent to the oracle are come
An hour since: Cleomenes and Dion,
Being well arriv'd from Delphos, are both landed,
Hasting to the court.

First Lord. So please you, sir, their speed
Hath been beyond account.

Leon. Twenty-three days 197
They have been absent: 'tis good speed; foretells
The great Apollo suddenly will have
The truth of this appear. Prepare you, lords;
Summon a session, that we may arraign 201
Our most disloyal lady; for, as she hath
Been publicly accus'd, so shall she have
A just and open trial. While she lives 204
My heart will be a burden to me. Leave me,
And think upon my bidding. *Exeunt.*

ACT THIRD

Scene One

[*A Town in Sicilia*]

Enter Cleomenes and Dion.

Cleo. The climate 's delicate, the air most sweet,
Fertile the isle, the temple much surpassing
The common praise it bears.

Dion. I shall report,

197 beyond account: *unaccountable* 199 suddenly: *promptly*

For most it caught me, the celestial habits,— 4
Methinks I so should term them,—and the reverence
Of the grave wearers. O, the sacrifice!
How ceremonious, solemn, and unearthly
It was i' the offering!
Cleo. But of all, the burst 8
And the ear-deafening voice o' the oracle,
Kin to Jove's thunder, so surpris'd my sense,
That I was nothing.
Dion. If the event o' the journey
Prove as successful to the queen,—O, be 't so!—
As it hath been to us rare, pleasant, speedy, 13
The time is worth the use on 't.
Cleo. Great Apollo
Turn all to the best! These proclamations,
So forcing faults upon Hermione, 16
I little like.
Dion. The violent carriage of it
Will clear or end the business: when the oracle,
Thus by Apollo's great divine seal'd up,
Shall the contents discover, something rare 20
Even then will rush to knowledge.—[*To an Attendant.*] Go:—fresh horses!
And gracious be the issue! *Exeunt.*

Scene Two

[*A Court of Justice*]

Enter Leontes, Lords, Officers.

Leon. This sessions, to our great grief we pronounce,
Even pushes 'gainst our heart: the party tried

4 habits: *garments* 11 event: *outcome*
17 carriage: *management* 22 gracious: *favorable*

The daughter of a king, our wife, and one
Of us too much belov'd. Let us be clear'd 4
Of being tyrannous, since we so openly
Proceed in justice, which shall have due course,
Even to the guilt or the purgation.
Produce the prisoner. 8

Offi. It is his highness' pleasure that the queen
Appear in person here in court. Silence!

[*Enter Hermione guarded; Paulina and Ladies attending.*]

Leon. Read the indictment. 11

Offi. [*Reads.*] 'Hermione, queen to the worthy Leontes, King of Sicilia, thou art here accused and arraigned of high treason, in committing adultery with Polixenes, King of Bohemia, and conspiring with Camillo to take away the life of our sovereign lord the king, thy royal husband: the pretence whereof being by circumstances 18 partly laid open, thou, Hermione, contrary to the faith and allegiance of a true subject, didst counsel and aid them, for their better safety, to fly away by night.'

Her. Since what I am to say must be but that
Which contradicts my accusation, and 24
The testimony on my part no other
But what comes from myself, it shall scarce boot me
To say 'Not guilty:' mine integrity
Being counted falsehood, shall, as I express it,
Be so receiv'd. But thus: if powers divine 29
Behold our human actions, as they do,
I doubt not then but innocence shall make
False accusation blush, and tyranny 32

7 purgation: *acquittal* 18 pretence: *purpose, design* 26 boot: *profit*

Tremble at patience. You, my lord, best know,—
Who least will seem to do so,—my past life
Hath been as continent, as chaste, as true,
As I am now unhappy; which is more 36
Than history can pattern, though devis'd
And play'd to take spectators. For behold me,
A fellow of the royal bed, which owe
A moiety of the throne, a great king's daughter,
The mother to a hopeful prince, here standing
To prate and talk for life and honour 'fore
Who please to come and hear. For life, I prize it
As I weigh grief, which I would spare: for honour, 44
'Tis a derivative from me to mine,
And only that I stand for. I appeal
To your own conscience, sir, before Polixenes
Came to your court, how I was in your grace, 48
How merited to be so; since he came,
With what encounter so uncurrent I
Have strain'd, to appear thus: if one jot beyond
The bound of honour, or in act or will 52
That way inclining, harden'd be the hearts
Of all that hear me, and my near'st of kin
Cry fie upon my grave!

Leon. I ne'er heard yet
That any of these bolder vices wanted 56
Less impudence to gainsay what they did
Than to perform it first.

Her. That 's true enough;
Though 'tis a saying, sir, not due to me.

Leon. You will not own it.

37 pattern: *give examples of* 38 take: *bewitch, fascinate*
39 owe: *own* 41 hopeful: *inspiring hope*
50 encounter: *behavior* uncurrent: *extraordinary*
51 strain'd: *transgressed beyond due limits* 57 gainsay: *deny*

Her. More than mistress of 60
Which comes to me in name of fault, I must not
At all acknowledge. For Polixenes,—
With whom I am accus'd,—I do confess
I lov'd him as in honour he requir'd, 64
With such a kind of love as might become
A lady like me; with a love even such,
So and no other, as yourself commanded:
Which not to have done I think had been in me
Both disobedience and ingratitude 69
To you and toward your friend, whose love had spoke,
Even since it could speak, from an infant, freely
That it was yours. Now, for conspiracy, 72
I know not how it tastes, though it be dish'd
For me to try how: all I know of it
Is that Camillo was an honest man;
And why he left your court, the gods themselves,
Wotting no more than I, are ignorant. 77
Leon. You knew of his departure, as you know
What you have underta'en to do in 's absence.
Her. Sir, 80
You speak a language that I understand not:
My life stands in the level of your dreams,
Which I'll lay down.
Leon. Your actions are my dreams:
You had a bastard by Polixenes, 84
And I but dream'd it. As you were past all shame,—
Those of your fact are so,—so past all truth:
Which to deny concerns more than avails; for as
Thy brat hath been cast out, like to itself, 88
No father owning it,—which is, indeed,
More criminal in thee than it,—so thou

60-62 More . . . acknowledge; *cf. n.*
77 Wotting: *knowing* 82 *Cf. n.* 86 fact: *deed*
87 concerns more than avails: *is more significant than helpful to you*

Shalt feel our justice, in whose easiest passage
Look for no less than death.
Her. Sir, spare your threats: 92
The bug which you would fright me with I seek.
To me can life be no commodity:
The crown and comfort of my life, your favour,
I do give lost; for I do feel it gone, 96
But know not how it went. My second joy,
And first-fruits of my body, from his presence
I am barr'd, like one infectious. My third comfort,
Starr'd most unluckily, is from my breast, 100
The innocent milk in its most innocent mouth,
Hal'd out to murder: myself on every post
Proclaim'd a strumpet: with immodest hatred
The child-bed privilege denied, which 'longs 104
To women of all fashion: lastly, hurried
Here to this place, i' the open air, before
I have got strength of limit. Now, my liege,
Tell me what blessings I have here alive, 108
That I should fear to die? Therefore proceed.
But yet hear this; mistake me not; no life,
I prize it not a straw:—but for mine honour,
Which I would free, if I shall be condemn'd 112
Upon surmises, all proofs sleeping else
But what your jealousies awake, I tell you
'Tis rigour and not law. Your honours all,
I do refer me to the oracle: 116
Apollo be my judge!
First Lord. This your request
Is altogether just: therefore, bring forth,
And in Apollo's name, his oracle.

91 passage: *procedure* 93 bug: *bugbear* 94 commodity: *advantage*
100 Starr'd most unluckily: *born under stars of most evil influence*
103 immodest: *immoderate* 105 fashion: *kinds*
107 of limit: *from a limited, or normal, period of recuperation*

[*Exeunt certain Officers.*]

Her. The Emperor of Russia was my father:
O! that he were alive, and here beholding 121
His daughter's trial; that he did but see
The flatness of my misery; yet with eyes
Of pity, not revenge! 124

[*Enter Officers, with Cleomenes and Dion.*]

Offi. You here shall swear upon this sword of justice,
That you, Cleomenes and Dion, have
Been both at Delphos, and from thence have brought
This seal'd-up oracle, by the hand deliver'd 128
Of great Apollo's priest, and that since then
You have not dar'd to break the holy seal,
Nor read the secrets in 't.

Cleo.
Dion. } All this we swear.

Leon. Break up the seals, and read. 132

Offi. [*Reads.*] 'Hermione is chaste; Polixenes blameless; Camillo a true subject; Leontes a jealous tyrant; his innocent babe truly begotten; and the king shall live without an heir if that which is lost be not found.' 137

Lords. Now blessed be the great Apollo!

Her. Praised!

Leon. Hast thou read truth?

Offi. Ay, my lord; even so
As it is here set down.

Leon. There is no truth at all i' the oracle: 141
The sessions shall proceed: this is mere falsehood.

[*Enter a Servant.*]

123 flatness: *absoluteness* 142 mere: *pure*

Ser. My lord the king, the king!
Leon. What is the business?
Ser. O sir! I shall be hated to report it: 144
The prince your son, with mere conceit and fear
Of the queen's speed, is gone.
Leon. How! gone!
Ser. Is dead.
Leon. Apollo 's angry; and the heavens themselves
Do strike at my injustice. [*Hermione swoons.*]
How now, there! 148
Paul. This news is mortal to the queen:—look down,
And see what death is doing.
Leon. Take her hence:
Her heart is but o'ercharg'd; she will recover:
I have too much believ'd mine own suspicion:
Beseech you, tenderly apply to her 153
Some remedies for life.—
[*Exeunt Paulina and Ladies, with Hermione.*]
Apollo, pardon
My great profaneness 'gainst thine oracle!
I'll reconcile me to Polixenes, 156
New woo my queen, recall the good Camillo,
Whom I proclaim a man of truth, of mercy;
For, being transported by my jealousies
To bloody thoughts and to revenge, I chose 160
Camillo for the minister to poison
My friend Polixenes: which had been done,
But that the good mind of Camillo tardied
My swift command; though I with death and with 164
Reward did threaten and encourage him,
Not doing it, and being done: he, most humane

145 conceit: *imagination* 146 speed: *fortune* 163 tardied: *delayed*

And fill'd with honour, to my kingly guest
Unclasp'd my practice, quit his fortunes here, 168
Which you knew great, and to the certain hazard
Of all incertainties himself commended,
No richer than his honour: how he glisters
Thorough my rust! and how his piety 172
Does my deeds make the blacker!

[*Enter Paulina.*]

Paul. Woe the while!
O, cut my lace, lest my heart, cracking it,
Break too!

First Lord. What fit is this, good lady?

Paul. What studied torments, tyrant, hast for me? 176
What wheels? racks? fires? What flaying? boiling
In leads, or oils? what old or newer torture
Must I receive, whose every word deserves
To taste of thy most worst? Thy tyranny, 180
Together working with thy jealousies,
Fancies too weak for boys, too green and idle
For girls of nine, O! think what they have done,
And then run mad indeed, stark mad; for all 184
Thy by-gone fooleries were but spices of it.
That thou betray'dst Polixenes, 'twas nothing;
That did but show thee of a fool, inconstant
And damnable ingrateful; nor was 't much 188
Thou wouldst have poison'd good Camillo's honour
To have him kill a king; poor trespasses,
More monstrous standing by: whereof I reckon
The casting forth to crows thy baby daughter 192

168 Unclasp'd: *revealed; cf. n.* practice: *plotting*
170 incertainties: *uncertain events* 171 glisters: *glitters*
172 Thorough: *through* 174 lace: *cord for lacing the bodice*
180 most worst: *worst* 185 spices: *foretastes* 187 of: *as*

To be or none or little; though a devil
Would have shed water out of fire ere done 't:
Nor is 't directly laid to thee, the death
Of the young prince, whose honourable thoughts,—
Thoughts high for one so tender,—cleft the heart
That could conceive a gross and foolish sire
Blemish'd his gracious dam: this is not, no,
Laid to thy answer: but the last,—O lords! 200
When I have said, cry, 'woe!'—the queen, the queen,
The sweetest, dearest creature 's dead, and vengeance for 't
Not dropp'd down yet.

First Lord. The higher powers forbid!

Paul. I say she 's dead; I'll swear 't: if word nor oath 204
Prevail not, go and see: if you can bring
Tincture or lustre in her lip, her eye,
Heat outwardly, or breath within, I'll serve you
As I would do the gods. But, O thou tyrant! 208
Do not repent these things, for they are heavier
Than all thy woes can stir; therefore betake thee
To nothing but despair. A thousand knees
Ten thousand years together, naked, fasting, 212
Upon a barren mountain, and still winter
In storm perpetual, could not move the gods
To look that way thou wert.

Leon. Go on, go on;
Thou canst not speak too much: I have deserv'd
All tongues to talk their bitterest.

First Lord. Say no more: 217
Howe'er the business goes, you have made fault
I' the boldness of your speech.

206 Tincture: *color*
210 stir: *i.e., remove from thy guilty record* 213 still: *always*

Paul. I am sorry for 't:
All faults I make, when I shall come to know them, 220
I do repent. Alas! I have show'd too much
The rashness of a woman: he is touch'd
To the noble heart. What 's gone and what 's past help
Should be past grief: do not receive affliction 224
At my petition; I beseech you, rather
Let me be punish'd, that have minded you
Of what you should forget. Now, good my liege,
Sir, royal sir, forgive a foolish woman: 228
The love I bore your queen,—lo, fool again!—
I'll speak of her no more, nor of your children;
I'll not remember you of my own lord,
Who is lost too: take your patience to you, 232
And I'll say nothing.

Leon. Thou didst speak but well,
When most the truth, which I receive much better
Than to be pitied of thee. Prithee, bring me
To the dead bodies of my queen and son: 236
One grave shall be for both: upon them shall
The causes of their death appear, unto
Our shame perpetual. Once a day I'll visit
The chapel where they lie, and tears shed there
Shall be my recreation: so long as nature 241
Will bear up with this exercise, so long
I daily vow to use it. Come and lead me
To these sorrows. *Exeunt.*

226 minded: *reminded* 231 remember: *remind*

Scene Three

[*Bohemia. A desert country near the sea*]

Enter Antigonus, [with the] Babe; and a Mariner.

Ant. Thou art perfect, then, our ship hath touch'd upon
The deserts of Bohemia?
Mar. Ay, my lord; and fear
We have landed in ill time: the skies look grimly
And threaten present blusters. In my conscience, 4
The heavens with that we have in hand are angry,
And frown upon 's.
Ant. Their sacred wills be done! Go, get aboard;
Look to thy bark: I'll not be long before 8
I call upon thee.
Mar. Make your best haste, and go not
Too far i' the land: 'tis like to be loud weather;
Besides, this place is famous for the creatures
Of prey that keep upon 't.
Ant. Go thou away: 12
I'll follow instantly.
Mar. I am glad at heart
To be so rid of the business. *Exit.*
Ant. Come, poor babe:
I have heard, but not believ'd, the spirits o' the dead
May walk again: if such thing be, thy mother 16
Appear'd to me last night, for ne'er was dream
So like a waking. To me comes a creature,
Sometimes her head on one side, some another;
I never saw a vessel of like sorrow, 20
So fill'd, and so becoming: in pure white robes,
Like very sanctity, she did approach

1 perfect: *certain* 4 blusters: *storms* 12 keep: *live*

My cabin where I lay; thrice bow'd before me,
And, gasping to begin some speech, her eyes 24
Became two spouts: the fury spent, anon
Did this break from her: 'Good Antigonus,
Since fate, against thy better disposition,
Hath made thy person for the thrower-out 28
Of my poor babe, according to thine oath,
Places remote enough are in Bohemia,
There weep and leave it crying; and, for the babe
Is counted lost for ever, Perdita, 32
I prithee, call 't: for this ungentle business,
Put on thee by my lord, thou ne'er shalt see
Thy wife Paulina more': and so, with shrieks,
She melted into air. Affrighted much, 36
I did in time collect myself, and thought
This was so and no slumber. Dreams are toys;
Yet for this once, yea, superstitiously,
I will be squar'd by this. I do believe 40
Hermione hath suffer'd death; and that
Apollo would, this being indeed the issue
Of King Polixenes, it should here be laid,
Either for life or death, upon the earth 44
Of its right father. Blossom, speed thee well!
[*Laying down Babe.*]
There lie; and there thy character: there these;
[*Laying down a bundle.*]
Which may, if fortune please, both breed thee, pretty,
And still rest thine. The storm begins: poor
wretch! 48
That for thy mother's fault art thus expos'd
To loss and what may follow. Weep I cannot,

31 for: *because*
39 superstitiously: *with religious reverence*
46 character: *written means of identification*
47, 48 Which . . . thine; *cf. n.*
38 toys: *trifles*
40 squar'd: *ruled*

But my heart bleeds, and most accurs'd am I
To be by oath enjoin'd to this. Farewell! 52
The day frowns more and more: thou art like to have
A lullaby too rough. I never saw
The heavens so dim by day. A savage clamour!
Well may I get aboard! This is the chase: 56
I am gone for ever. *Exit, pursued by a bear.*

[*Enter a Shepherd.*]

Shep. I would there were no age between ten and three-and-twenty, or that youth would sleep out the rest; for there is nothing in the between but getting wenches with child, wronging the ancientry, stealing, fighting. Hark you now! Would any but these boiled brains 63 of nineteen and two-and-twenty hunt this weather? They have scared away two of my best sheep; which I fear the wolf will sooner find than the master: if anywhere I have them, 'tis by the sea-side, browsing of ivy. Good luck, an 't be thy will! what have we here? Mercy on 's, a barne; a very pretty barne! A boy 70 or a child, I wonder? A pretty one, a very pretty one; sure some scape: though I am not bookish, yet I can read waiting-gentlewoman in the scape. This has been some stair-work, some trunk-work, some behind-door-work; they were warmer that got this than the poor thing is here. I'll take it up for pity; yet I'll tarry till my son come; he hollaed but even now. Whoa, ho, hoa! 79

Enter Clown.

56 the chase: *a hunted wild beast* 59 ten; *cf. n.*
62 ancientry: *old people* 63 boiled brains: *hot heads*
70 barne: *child* 71 child: *girl* 72 scape: *transgression*
79 S. d. Clown: *country bumpkin*

Clo. Hilloa, loa!

Shep. What! art so near? If thou 'lt see a thing to talk on when thou art dead and rotten, come hither. What ailest thou, man? 83

Clo. I have seen two such sights by sea and by land! but I am not to say it is a sea, for it is now the sky: betwixt the firmament and it you cannot thrust a bodkin's point.

Shep. Why, boy, how is it? 88

Clo. I would you did but see how it chafes, how it rages, how it takes up the shore! but that 's not to the point. O! the most piteous cry of the poor souls; sometimes to see 'em, and not to see 'em; now the ship boring the moon with her mainmast, and anon swallowed with yest and froth, as you 'd thrust a cork into a hogshead. And then for the land-service: to 96 see how the bear tore out his shoulderbone; how he cried to me for help and said his name was Antigonus, a nobleman. But to make an end of the ship: to see how the sea flap-dragoned it: but, first, how the poor souls roared, and the sea mocked them; and how the poor gentleman roared, and the bear mocked him, both roaring louder than the sea or weather. 104

Shep. Name of mercy! when was this, boy?

Clo. Now, now; I have not winked since I saw these sights: the men are not yet cold under water, nor the bear half dined on the gentleman: he 's at it now. 109

87 bodkin: *small pointed instrument* 95 yest: *foam*
96 land-service: *military, as compared with naval, service; used humorously*
100 flap-dragoned; *cf. n.*

Shep. Would I had been by, to have helped the old man!

Clo. I would you had been by the ship's side, to have helped her: there your charity would have lacked footing. 114

Shep. Heavy matters! heavy matters! but look thee here, boy. Now bless thyself: thou mettest with things dying, I with things new born. Here 's a sight for thee; look thee, a bearing-cloth for a squire's child! Look thee here: take up, take up, boy; open 't. So, let 's see: it was told me, I should be rich by the fairies: this is some changeling.—Open 't. What 's within, boy? 123

Clo. You're a made old man: if the sins of your youth are forgiven you, you're well to live. Gold! all gold!

Shep. This is fairy gold, boy, and 'twill prove so: up with 't, keep it close: home, home, the next way. We are lucky, boy; and to be so 129 still, requires nothing but secrecy. Let my sheep go. Come, good boy, the next way home.

Clo. Go you the next way with your findings. I'll go see if the bear be gone from the gentleman, and how much he hath eaten: they are never curst but when they are hungry. If there be any of him left, I'll bury it. 136

Shep. That 's a good deed. If thou mayst discern by that which is left of him what he is, fetch me to the sight of him.

119 bearing-cloth: *infant's christening robe* squire's: *gentleman's*
122 changeling: *elfin child left by fairies in place of stolen human one*
125 well to live: *well to do* 129 next: *nearest* 135 curst: *savage*

Clo. Marry, will I; and you shall help to put him i' the ground. 141

Shep. 'Tis a lucky day, boy, and we'll do good deeds on 't. *Exeunt.*

ACT FOURTH

Scene One

Enter Time, the Chorus.

Time. I, that please some, try all, both joy and terror
Of good and bad, that make and unfold error,
Now take upon me, in the name of Time,
To use my wings. Impute it not a crime 4
To me or my swift passage, that I slide
O'er sixteen years, and leave the growth untried
Of that wide gap; since it is in my power
To o'erthrow law, and in one self-born hour 8
To plant and o'erwhelm custom. Let me pass
The same I am, ere ancient'st order was
Or what is now receiv'd: I witness to
The times that brought them in; so shall I do
To the freshest things now reigning, and make stale 13
The glistering of this present, as my tale
Now seems to it. Your patience this allowing,
I turn my glass and give my scene such growing 16
As you had slept between. Leontes leaving,—
The effects of his fond jealousies so grieving,
That he shuts up himself,—imagine me,

140 Marry: *an exclamation, from the name of the Virgin Mary*
8 one self-born: *one and the self-same*
11 receiv'd: *accepted* 18 grieving: *grieving over*

Gentle spectators, that I now may be 20
In fair Bohemia; and remember well,
I mention'd a son o' the king's, which Florizel
I now name to you; and with speed so pace
To speak of Perdita, now grown in grace 24
Equal with wondering: what of her ensues
I list not prophesy; but let Time's news
Be known when 'tis brought forth. A shepherd's daughter,
And what to her adheres, which follows after,
Is th' argument of Time. Of this allow, 29
If ever you have spent time worse ere now:
If never, yet that Time himself doth say
He wishes earnestly you never may. *Exit.*

Scene Two

[Bohemia. A Room in the Palace of Polixenes]

Enter Polixenes and Camillo.

Pol. I pray thee, good Camillo, be no more importunate: 'tis a sickness denying thee anything; a death to grant this. 3

Cam. It is fifteen years since I saw my country: though I have for the most part been aired abroad, I desire to lay my bones there. Besides, the penitent king, my master, hath sent for me; to whose feeling sorrows I might be some allay, or I o'erween to think so, which is another spur to my departure. 10

Pol. As thou lovest me, Camillo, wipe not out the rest of thy services by leaving me now.

25 Equal with wondering: *as much as in admiration* 26 list: *wish to*
28 adheres: *is related* 29 argument: *subject-matter*
5 been aired: *lived* 8 feeling: *deeply felt*
9 o'erween: *rate myself too highly*

The need I have of thee thine own goodness hath made: better not to have had thee than thus to want thee. Thou, having made me businesses which none without thee can sufficiently manage, must either stay to execute them thyself or take away with thee the very services thou hast done; which if I have not enough considered,—as too much I cannot,—to be more thankful to thee 20 shall be my study, and my profit therein, the heaping friendships. Of that fatal country, Sicilia, prithee speak no more, whose very naming punishes me with the remembrance of that penitent, as thou callest him, and reconciled king, my brother; whose loss of his most precious queen and children are even now to be afresh lamented. Say to me, when sawest thou the Prince Florizel, my son? Kings are no less unhappy, their issue not being gracious, than they are in losing them when they have approved their virtues. 30

Cam. Sir, it is three days since I saw the prince. What his happier affairs may be, are to me unknown; but I have missingly noted he is of late much retired from court, and is less frequent to his princely exercises than formerly he hath appeared. 37

Pol. I have considered so much, Camillo, and with some care; so far, that I have eyes under my service which look upon his removedness; from whom I have this intelligence, that he is seldom from the house of a most homely shepherd; a man, they say, that from very nothing,

22 heaping friendships: *increase of friendly acts*
30 gracious: *upright, righteous* 31 approved: *tested*
34 missingly: *grieving at his absence*
40 removedness: *absence* 41 intelligence: *news*

and beyond the imagination of his neighbours, is grown into an unspeakable estate. 45

Cam. I have heard, sir, of such a man, who hath a daughter of most rare note: the report of her is extended more than can be thought to begin from such a cottage. 49

Pol. That 's likewise part of my intelligence; but, I fear, the angle that plucks our son thither. Thou shalt accompany us to the place; where we will, not appearing what we are, have some question with the shepherd; from whose simplicity I think it not uneasy to get the cause of my son's resort thither. Prithee, be my present partner in this business, and lay aside the thoughts of Sicilia. 58

Cam. I willingly obey your command.

Pol. My best Camillo!—We must disguise ourselves. *Exeunt.*

Scene Three

[*A Road near the Shepherd's Cottage*]

Enter Autolycus, singing.

'When daffodils begin to peer,
With heigh! the doxy, over the dale,
Why, then comes in the sweet o' the year;
For the red blood reigns in the winter's pale. 4

'The white sheet bleaching on the hedge,
With heigh! the sweet birds, O, how they sing!
Doth set my pugging tooth on edge;
For a quart of ale is a dish for a king. 8

47 note: *celebrity* 51 angle: *fish-hook* 54 question: *conversation*
1 peer: *show slightly* 2 doxy: *beggar's mistress*
4 winter's pale; *cf. n.* 7 pugging: *thieving*

'The lark, that tirra-lirra chants,
With, heigh! with, heigh! the thrush and the jay,
Are summer songs for me and my aunts,
While we lie tumbling in the hay.' 12

I have served Prince Florizel, and in my time wore three-pile; but now I am out of service:

'But shall I go mourn for that, my dear?
The pale moon shines by night; 16
And when I wander here and there,
I then do most go right.

'If tinkers may have leave to live,
And bear the sow-skin bowget, 20
Then my account I well may give,
And in the stocks avouch it.'

My traffic is sheets; when the kite builds, look to lesser linen. My father named me Autolycus; who being, as I am, littered under Mercury, was likewise a snapper-up of unconsidered trifles. With die and drab I purchased this caparison, 27 and my revenue is the silly cheat. Gallows and knock are too powerful on the highway: beating and hanging are terrors to me: for the life to come, I sleep out the thought of it. A prize! a prize! 32

Enter Clown.

Clo. Let me see: Every 'leven wether tods;

11 aunts: *mistresses (thieves' slang)*
14 three-pile: *most costly kind of velvet*
20 bowget: *budget, big wallet*
23 *Cf. n.*
25 littered under Mercury; *cf. n.*
27 *By means of dice and lewd women I acquired this clothing*
28 silly cheat: *petty thieving* gallows and knock: *fear of hanging and of the officer's blow*
33 tods: *yields a tod, twenty-eight pounds of wool*

every tod yields pound and odd shilling: fifteen hundred shorn, what comes the wool to?

Aut. [*Aside.*] If the springe hold, the cock 's mine. 37

Clo. I cannot do 't without compters. Let me see; what am I to buy for our sheep-shearing feast? 'Three pound of sugar; five pound of currants; rice,' what will this sister of mine do with rice? But my father hath made her mistress of the feast, and she lays it on. She hath made me four-and-twenty nosegays for the shearers, three-man song-men all, and very good ones; but they are most of them means and basses: but one puritan amongst them, and 47 he sings psalms to hornpipes. I must have saffron, to colour the warden pies; mace, dates,—none; that 's out of my note:—nutmegs seven; a race or two of ginger,—but that I may beg;—four pound of prunes, and as many of raisins o' the sun. 53

Aut. O! that ever I was born!

[*Grovelling on the ground.*]

Clo. I' the name of me!—

Aut. O! help me, help me! pluck but off these rags, and then death, death! 57

Clo. Alack, poor soul! thou hast need of more rags to lay on thee, rather than have these off. 60

36 springe: *bird-hunter's noose* cock: *woodcock, a slang term for a fool*
38 compters: *pieces of metal used in making calculations*
43 lays it on: *manages lavishly*
45 three-man song-men: *singers of songs in three parts*
46 means: *altos* 47 puritan; *cf. n.*
48 saffron: *orange-red substance used for coloring cookery*
49 warden: *made of the warden pear* 50 note: *list*
51 race: *root* 52 raisins o' the sun: *sun-dried grapes*

Aut. O, sir! the loathsomeness of them offends me more than the stripes I have received, which are mighty ones and millions.

Clo. Alas, poor man! a million of beating may come to a great matter. 65

Aut. I am robbed, sir, and beaten; my money and apparel ta'en from me, and these detestable things put upon me. 68

Clo. What, by a horseman or a footman?

Aut. A footman, sweet sir, a footman.

Clo. Indeed, he should be a footman, by the garments he hath left with thee: if this be a horseman's coat, it hath seen very hot service. Lend me thy hand, I'll help thee: come, lend me thy hand. [*Helping him up.*]

Aut. O! good sir, tenderly, O! 76

Clo. Alas, poor soul!

Aut. O! good sir; softly, good sir! I fear, sir, my shoulder-blade is out.

Clo. How now! canst stand? 80

Aut. Softly, dear sir; [*Picks his pocket.*] good sir, softly. You ha' done me a charitable office.

Clo. Dost lack any money? I have a little money for thee. 84

Aut. No, good sweet sir: no, I beseech you, sir. I have a kinsman not past three-quarters of a mile hence, unto whom I was going: I shall there have money, or anything I want: offer me no money, I pray you! that kills my heart. 89

Clo. What manner of fellow was he that robbed you?

Aut. A fellow, sir, that I have known to go about with trol-my-dames: I knew him once a

93 trol-my-dames: *a game in which balls were 'trolled' through arches set on a board*

servant of the prince. I cannot tell, good sir, for which of his virtues it was, but he was certainly whipped out of the court. 96

Clo. His vices, you would say: there 's no virtue whipped out of the court: they cherish it, to make it stay there, and yet it will no more but abide. 100

Aut. Vices, I would say, sir. I know this man well: he hath been since an ape-bearer; then a process-server, a bailiff; then he compassed a motion of the Prodigal Son, and married a tinker's wife within a mile where my land and living lies; and having flown over many knavish professions, he settled only in rogue: some call him Autolycus. 108

Clo. Out upon him! Prig, for my life, prig: he haunts wakes, fairs, and bear-baitings.

Aut. Very true, sir; he, sir, he: that 's the rogue that put me into this apparel. 112

Clo. Not a more cowardly rogue in all Bohemia: if you had but looked big and spit at him, he'd have run.

Aut. I must confess to you, sir, I am no fighter: I am false of heart that way, and that he knew, I warrant him. 118

Clo. How do you now?

Aut. Sweet sir, much better than I was: I can stand and walk. I will even take my leave of you, and pace softly towards my kinsman's.

Clo. Shall I bring thee on the way?

Aut. No, good-faced sir; no, sweet sir. 124

99 no more but abide: *barely make a brief stay*
102 ape-bearer: *showman who carries a trained monkey*
103 compassed: *acquired* 104 motion: *puppet show* 109 Prig: *thief*

Clo. Then fare thee well: I must go buy spices for our sheep-shearing. *Exit.*

Aut. Prosper you, sweet sir! Your purse is not hot enough to purchase your spice. I'll be with you at your sheep-shearing too. If I make not this cheat bring out another, and the shearers prove sheep, let me be unrolled, and my name put in the book of virtue. 132

Song. 'Jog on, jog on, the footpath way,
And merrily hent the stile-a:
A merry heart goes all the day,
Your sad tires in a mile-a.' *Exit.*

Scene Four

[*A Lawn before the Shepherd's Cottage*]

Enter Florizel and Perdita.

Flo. These your unusual weeds to each part of you
Do give a life: no shepherdess, but Flora
Peering in April's front. This your sheep-shearing
Is as a meeting of the petty gods, 4
And you the queen on 't.

Per. Sir, my gracious lord,
To chide at your extremes it not becomes me:
O! pardon, that I name them. Your high self,
The gracious mark o' the land, you have obscur'd 8
With a swain's wearing, and me, poor lowly maid,
Most goddess-like prank'd up. But that our feasts
In every mess have folly, and the feeders

131 unrolled: *stricken from the roll of thieves* 134 hent: *get over*
1 weeds: *garments* 3 Peering: *appearing* front: *van or beginning*
6 extremes: *extravagances of conduct*
8 mark o' the land: *landmark or model of the nation*
9 wearing: *clothing* 10 prank'd up: *decked out*

Digest it with a custom, I should blush 12
To see you so attired,—swoon, I think,
To show myself a glass.

Flo. I bless the time
When my good falcon made her flight across
Thy father's ground.

Per. Now, Jove afford you cause! 16
To me the difference forges dread: your greatness
Hath not been us'd to fear. Even now I tremble
To think, your father, by some accident,
Should pass this way as you did. O, the Fates!
How would he look, to see his work, so noble, 21
Vilely bound up? What would he say? Or how
Should I, in these my borrow'd flaunts, behold
The sternness of his presence?

Flo. Apprehend 24
Nothing but jollity. The gods themselves,
Humbling their deities to love, have taken
The shapes of beasts upon them: Jupiter
Became a bull, and bellow'd; the green Neptune
A ram, and bleated; and the fire-rob'd god, 29
Golden Apollo, a poor humble swain,
As I seem now. Their transformations
Were never for a piece of beauty rarer, 32
Nor in a way so chaste, since my desires
Run not before mine honour, nor my lusts
Burn hotter than my faith.

Per. O! but, sir,
Your resolution cannot hold, when 'tis 36
Oppos'd, as it must be, by the power of the king.
One of these two must be necessities,

12 with a custom: *from force of habit* 13 swoon; *cf. n.*
17 difference: *difference in rank*
23 flaunts: *finery* 27-30 *Cf. n.* 35 faith: *fidelity*

Which then will speak, that you must change this purpose,
Or I my life.

Flo. Thou dearest Perdita, 40
With these forc'd thoughts, I prithee, darken not
The mirth o' the feast: or I'll be thine, my fair,
Or not my father's; for I cannot be
Mine own, nor anything to any, if 44
I be not thine: to this I am most constant,
Though destiny say no. Be merry, gentle;
Strangle such thoughts as these with anything
That you behold the while. Your guests are coming: 48
Lift up your countenance, as it were the day
Of celebration of that nuptial which
We two have sworn shall come.

Per. O lady Fortune,
Stand you auspicious!

Flo. See, your guests approach: 52
Address yourself to entertain them sprightly,
And let 's be red with mirth.

[*Enter Shepherd, with Polixenes and Camillo disguised; Clown, Mopsa, Dorcas, and Others.*]

Shep. Fie, daughter! when my old wife liv'd, upon
This day she was both pantler, butler, cook; 56
Both dame and servant; welcom'd all, serv'd all,
Would sing her song and dance her turn; now here,
At upper end o' the table, now i' the middle;
On his shoulder, and his; her face o' fire 60
With labour and the thing she took to quench it,
She would to each one sip. You are retir'd,

41 forc'd: *unnatural*
53 Address yourself: *make ready* sprightly: *in sprightly manner*
56 pantler: *servant in charge of pantry*

As if you were a feasted one and not
The hostess of the meeting: pray you, bid 64
These unknown friends to 's welcome; for it is
A way to make us better friends, more known.
Come, quench your blushes and present yourself
That which you are, mistress o' the feast: come on, 68
And bid us welcome to your sheep-shearing,
As your good flock shall prosper.

Per. [*To Polixenes.*] Sir, welcome:
It is my father's will I should take on me
The hostess-ship o' the day. [*To Camillo.*] You're welcome, sir. 72
Give me those flowers there, Dorcas. Reverend sirs,
For you there 's rosemary and rue; these keep
Seeming and savour all the winter long:
Grace and remembrance be to you both, 76
And welcome to our shearing!

Pol. Shepherdess,—
A fair one are you,—well you fit our ages
With flowers of winter.

Per. Sir, the year growing ancient,
Not yet on summer's death, nor on the birth 80
Of trembling winter, the fairest flowers o' the season
Are our carnations, and streak'd gillyvors,
Which some call nature's bastards: of that kind
Our rustic garden 's barren, and I care not 84
To get slips of them.

Pol. Wherefore, gentle maiden,
Do you neglect them?

Per. For I have heard it said

75 Seeming: *beauty of shape* savour: *fragrance*
76 Grace and remembrance; *cf. n.*
82 gillyvors: *gillyflowers, pinks* (?)

There is an art which in their piedness shares
With great creating nature.

Pol. Say there be; 88
Yet nature is made better by no mean
But nature makes that mean: so, over that art,
Which you say adds to nature, is an art
That nature makes. You see, sweet maid, we marry 92
A gentler scion to the wildest stock,
And make conceive a bark of baser kind
By bud of nobler race: this is an art
Which does mend nature, change it rather, but
The art itself is nature.

Per. So it is. 97

Pol. Then make your garden rich in gillyvors,
And do not call them bastards.

Per. I'll not put
The dibble in earth to set one slip of them; 100
No more than, were I painted, I would wish
This youth should say, 'twere well, and only therefore
Desire to breed by me. Here's flowers for you;
Hot lavender, mints, savory, marjoram; 104
The marigold, that goes to bed wi' the sun,
And with him rises weeping: these are flowers
Of middle summer, and I think they are given
To men of middle age. You're very welcome. 108

Cam. I should leave grazing, were I of your flock,
And only live by gazing.

Per. Out, alas!
You'd be so lean, that blasts of January
Would blow you through and through. Now, my fair'st friend, 112

87, 88 There . . . nature; *cf. n.* 89 mean: *instrument*
100 dibble: *gardener's tool to make holes for planting* 104 *Cf. n.*

I would I had some flowers o' the spring that might
Become your time of day; and yours, and yours,
That wear upon your virgin branches yet
Your maidenheads growing: O Proserpina! 116
For the flowers now that frighted thou let'st fall
From Dis's waggon! daffodils,
That come before the swallow dares, and take
The winds of March with beauty; violets dim,
But sweeter than the lids of Juno's eyes 121
Or Cytherea's breath; pale primroses,
That die unmarried, ere they can behold
Bright Phœbus in his strength, a malady 124
Most incident to maids; bold oxlips and
The crown imperial; lilies of all kinds,
The flower-de-luce being one. O! these I lack
To make you garlands of, and my sweet friend,
To strew him o'er and o'er!

Flo. What! like a corse? 129

Per. No, like a bank for love to lie and play on;
Not like a corse; or if,—not to be buried,
But quick and in mine arms. Come, take your flowers: 132
Methinks I play as I have seen them do
In Whitsun pastorals: sure this robe of mine
Does change my disposition.

Flo. What you do
Still betters what is done. When you speak, sweet, 136
I'd have you do it ever: when you sing,
I'd have you buy and sell so; so give alms;

116 Proserpina; *cf. n.*
122 Cytherea's: *Venus's*
126 crown imperial: *an imported flower from Asia Minor, the fritillaria imperialis*
127 flower-de-luce: *iris*
132 quick: *alive*
134 Whitsun pastorals; *cf. n.*

Pray so; and, for the ordering your affairs,
To sing them too: when you do dance, I wish you 140
A wave o' the sea, that you might ever do
Nothing but that; move still, still so,
And own no other function: each your doing,
So singular in each particular, 144
Crowns what you are doing in the present deed,
That all your acts are queens.

Per. O Doricles!
Your praises are too large: but that your youth,
And the true blood which fairly peeps through it,
Do plainly give you out an unstain'd shepherd,
With wisdom I might fear, my Doricles,
You woo'd me the false way.

Flo. I think you have
As little skill to fear as I have purpose 152
To put you to 't. But, come; our dance, I pray.
Your hand, my Perdita: so turtles pair
That never mean to part.

Per. I'll swear for 'em.

Pol. This is the prettiest low-born lass that ever 156
Ran on the green-sord: nothing she does or seems
But smacks of something greater than herself;
Too noble for this place.

Cam. He tells her something
That makes her blood look out. Good sooth, she is 160
The queen of curds and cream.

Clo. Come on, strike up.

143 each your doing: *each act of yours*
144 singular: *characteristic of you, unique* particular: *detail*
147 large: *extravagant*
149 give you out: *declare you*
152 skill: *reason*
154 turtles: *turtle-doves*
157 sord: *sward*
160 sooth: *truth*

Dor. Mopsa must be your mistress: marry, garlic,
To mend her kissing with.

Mop. Now, in good time!

Clo. Not a word, a word: we stand upon our manners. 164
Come, strike up. [*Music.*]

Here a dance of Shepherds and Shepherdesses.

Pol. Pray, good shepherd, what fair swain is this
Which dances with your daughter?

Shep. They call him Doricles, and boasts himself 168
To have a worthy feeding; but I have it
Upon his own report and I believe it:
He looks like sooth. He says he loves my daughter:
I think so too; for never gaz'd the moon 172
Upon the water as he'll stand and read
As 'twere my daughter's eyes; and, to be plain,
I think there is not half a kiss to choose
Who loves another best.

Pol. She dances featly. 176

Shep. So she does anything, though I report it
That should be silent. If young Doricles
Do light upon her, she shall bring him that
Which he not dreams of. 180

Enter a Servant.

Serv. O master! if you did but hear the pedlar at the door, you would never dance again after a tabor and pipe; no, the bagpipe could not move you. He sings several tunes faster than you'll tell money; he utters them as he had eaten ballads and all men's ears grew to his tunes. 186

169 feeding: *tract of pasture*
176 another: *the other* featly: *nimbly*
183 tabor: *small drum* 185 tell: *count* as: *as if*

Clo. He could never come better: he shall come in: I love a ballad but even too well, if it be doleful matter merrily set down, or a very pleasant thing indeed and sung lamentably. 190

Serv. He hath songs for man or woman, of all sizes; no milliner can so fit his customers with gloves: he has the prettiest love-songs for maids; so without bawdry, which is strange; with such delicate burdens of dildos and fadings, 'jump 195 her and thump her'; and where some stretch-mouthed rascal would, as it were, mean mischief and break a foul gap into the matter, he makes the maid to answer, 'Whoop, do me no harm, good man;' puts him off, slights him with 'Whoop, do me no harm, good man.' 201

Pol. This is a brave fellow.

Clo. Believe me, thou talkest of an admirable conceited fellow. Has he any unbraided wares?

Serv. He hath ribands of all the colours i' the rainbow; points more than all the lawyers in Bohemia can learnedly handle, though they come to him by the gross; inkles, caddisses, 208 cambrics, lawns: why, he sings 'em over, as they were gods or goddesses. You would think a smock were a she-angel, he so chants to the sleeve-hand and the work about the square on't.

Clo. Prithee, bring him in, and let him approach singing. 214

195 burdens: *refrains* 195, 196 *Cf. n.*
196 stretch-mouthed: *foul-mouthed* 202 brave: *fine*
203 admirable conceited: *wonderfully witty*
204 unbraided: *unfaded* 205 ribands: *ribbons*
206 points: *tags with lacings for fastening hose to doublet or jacket*
208 inkles: *broad linen tape* caddisses: *garters of worsted tape*
209 lawns: *fine silks* 211 smock: *woman's undergarment*
212 sleeve-hand: *cuff* work about the square: *embroidery about the bosom*

Per. Forewarn him that he use no scurrilous words in 's tunes. [*Exit Servant.*]

Clo. You have of these pedlars, that have more in them than you'd think, sister.

Per. Ay, good brother, or go about to think.

Enter Autolycus, singing.

'Lawn as white as driven snow; 220
Cyprus black as e'er was crow;
Gloves as sweet as damask roses;
Masks for faces and for noses;
Bugle-bracelet, necklace-amber, 224
Perfume for a lady's chamber;
Golden quoifs and stomachers,
For my lads to give their dears;
Pins and poking-sticks of steel; 228
What maids lack from head to heel:
Come buy of me, come; come buy, come buy;
Buy, lads, or else your lasses cry:
Come buy.' 232

Clo. If I were not in love with Mopsa, thou shouldst take no money of me; but being enthralled as I am, it will also be the bondage of certain ribands and gloves. 236

Mop. I was promised them against the feast; but they come not too late now.

Dor. He hath promised you more than that, or there be liars. 240

Mop. He hath paid you all he promised you:

217 You have of these: *there are some* 219 go about: *make an effort*
221 Cyprus: *crape* 222 sweet: *perfumed*
224 Bugle-bracelet: *bracelet of tube-shaped glass beads*
226 quoifs: *women's headdresses* stomachers: *ornamental coverings for bosom*
228 poking-sticks: *metal rods to adjust plaits of ruffs*
237 against: *in time for*

may be he has paid you more, which will shame you to give him again. 243

Clo. Is there no manners left among maids? will they wear their plackets where they should bear their faces? Is there not milking-time, when you are going to bed, or kiln-hole, to whistle off these secrets, but you must be tittle-tattling before all our guests? 'Tis well they are whispering: clamour your tongues, and not a word more.

Mop. I have done. Come, you promised me a tawdry lace and a pair of sweet gloves. 252

Clo. Have I not told thee how I was cozened by the way, and lost all my money?

Aut. And indeed, sir, there are cozeners abroad; therefore it behoves men to be wary. 256

Clo. Fear not thou, man, thou shalt lose nothing here.

Aut. I hope so, sir; for I have about me many parcels of charge. 260

Clo. What hast here? ballads?

Mop. Pray now, buy some: I love a ballad in print, a-life, for then we are sure they are true.

Aut. Here's one to a very doleful tune, how a usurer's wife was brought to bed of twenty money-bags at a burden; and how she longed to eat adders' heads and toads carbonadoed.

Mop. Is it true, think you? 268

Aut. Very true, and but a month old.

Dor. Bless me from marrying a usurer!

Aut. Here 's the midwife's name to 't, one Mis-

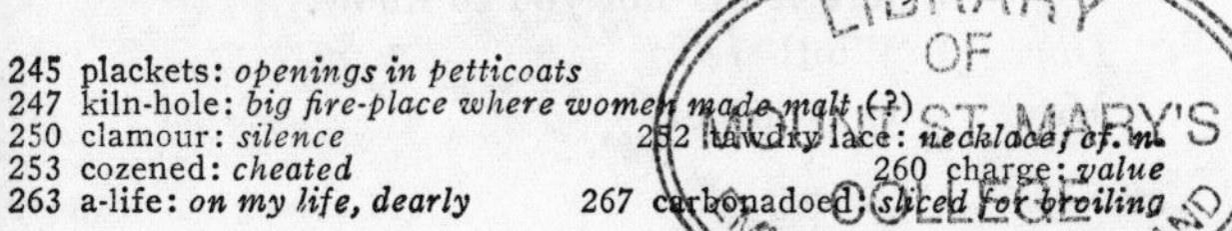
245 plackets: *openings in petticoats*
247 kiln-hole: *big fire-place where women made malt* (?)
250 clamour: *silence* 252 tawdry lace: *necklace; cf. n.*
253 cozened: *cheated* 260 charge: *value*
263 a-life: *on my life, dearly* 267 carbonadoed: *sliced for broiling*

tress Taleporter, and five or six honest wives' that were present. Why should I carry lies abroad?

Mop. Pray you now, buy it. 274

Clo. Come on, lay it by: and let 's first see moe ballads; we'll buy the other things anon.

Aut. Here 's another ballad of a fish that appeared upon the coast on Wednesday the fourscore of April, forty thousand fathom above water, and sung this ballad against the hard hearts of maids: it was thought she was a woman and was turned into a cold fish for she would not exchange flesh with one that loved her. The ballad is very pitiful and as true. 284

Dor. Is it true too, think you?

Aut. Five justices' hands at it, and witnesses more than my pack will hold.

Clo. Lay it by too: another. 288

Aut. This is a merry ballad, but a very pretty one.

Mop. Let 's have some merry ones.

Aut. Why, this is a passing merry one, and goes to the tune of 'Two maids wooing a man': there's scarce a maid westward but she sings it: 'tis in request, I can tell you. 295

Mop. We can both sing it: if thou 'lt bear a part thou shalt hear; 'tis in three parts.

Dor. We had the tune on 't a month ago.

Aut. I can bear my part; you must know 'tis my occupation: have at it with you. 300

Aut. 'Get you hence, for I must go,
Where it fits not you to know.'

Dor. 'Whither?'

Mop. 'O! whither?' 304

276 anon: *immediately* 292 passing: *surpassingly*

Dor. 'Whither?'
Mop. 'It becomes thy oath full well,
Thou to me thy secrets tell.'
Dor. 'Me too: let me go thither.' 308
Mop. 'Or thou go'st to the grange or mill.'
Dor. 'If to either, thou dost ill.'
Aut. 'Neither.'
Dor. 'What, neither?' 312
Aut. 'Neither.'
Dor. 'Thou hast sworn my love to be.'
Mop. 'Thou hast sworn it more to me:
Then whither go'st? say whither?' 316

Clo. We'll have this song out anon by ourselves: my father and the gentlemen are in sad talk, and we'll not trouble them: come, bring away thy pack after me. Wenches, I'll buy for you both. Pedlar, let's have the first choice. Follow me, girls. [*Exit with Dorcas and Mopsa.*]

Aut. And you shall pay well for 'em.

Song. 'Will you buy any tape, 324
Or lace for your cape,
My dainty duck, my dear-a?
Any silk, any thread,
Any toys for your head, 328
Of the new'st and fin'st, fin'st wear-a?
Come to the pedlar;
Money 's a meddler,
That doth utter all men's ware-a.' 332
Exit.

[*Enter a Servant.*]

Serv. Master, there is three carters, three

309 grange: *farmhouse* 318 sad: *serious* 320 Wenches: *girls*
331 meddler: *a go-between* 332 utter: *put in circulation, market*

shepherds, three neat-herds, three swine-herds, that have made themselves all men of hair; 335 they call themselves Saltiers; and they have a dance which the wenches say is a gallimaufry of gambols, because they are not in 't; but they themselves are o' the mind,—if it be not too rough for some that know little but bowling,— it will please plentifully. 341

Shep. Away! we'll none on 't: here has been too much homely foolery already. I know, sir, we weary you. 344

Pol. You weary those that refresh us: pray, let 's see these four threes of herdsmen.

Serv. One three of them, by their own report, sir, hath danced before the king; and not the worst of the three but jumps twelve foot and a half by the squier. 350

Shep. Leave your prating: since these good men are pleased, let them come in: but quickly now.

Serv. Why, they stay at door, sir.

Here a dance of twelve Satyrs.

Pol. [*To Shep.*] O father! you'll know more of that hereafter.
[*To Camillo.*] Is it not too far gone? 'Tis time to part them. 356
He 's simple and tells much. [*To Florizel.*] How now, fair shepherd!
Your heart is full of something that does take
Your mind from feasting. Sooth, when I was young,
And handed love as you do, I was wont 360

334 neat-herds: *cowherds*
335 men of hair: *men dressed as hairy satyrs*
336 Saltiers: *blunder for satyrs*
337 gallimaufry: *hotch-potch*
350 squier: *measure*
360 handed: *held the hand of*

To load my she with knacks: I would have ransack'd
The pedlar's silken treasury and have pour'd it
To her acceptance; you have let him go
And nothing marted with him. If your lass 364
Interpretation should abuse and call this
Your lack of love or bounty, you were straited
For a reply, at least if you make a care
Of happy holding her.

Flo. Old sir, I know 368
She prizes not such trifles as these are.
The gifts she looks from me are pack'd and lock'd
Up in my heart, which I have given already,
But not deliver'd. O! hear me breathe my life
Before this ancient sir, who, it should seem, 373
Hath sometime lov'd: I take thy hand; this hand,
As soft as dove's down, and as white as it,
Or Ethiopian's tooth, or the fann'd snow 376
That 's bolted by the northern blasts twice o'er.

Pol. What follows this?
How prettily the young swain seems to wash
The hand was fair before! I have put you out:
But to your protestation: let me hear 381
What you profess.

Flo. Do, and be witness to 't.

Pol. And this my neighbour too?

Flo. And he, and more
Than he, and men, the earth, the heavens, and all; 384
That, were I crown'd the most imperial monarch,
Thereof most worthy, were I the fairest youth
That ever made eye swerve, had force and knowledge
More than was ever man's, I would not prize
them 388

351 she: *lady* knacks: *knick-knacks* 364 marted: *traded*
365 Interpretation should abuse: *should misinterpret*
366 straited: *put in straits* 370 looks: *looks for* 377 bolted: *sifted*

Without her love: for her employ them all;
Commend them and condemn them to her service
Or to their own perdition.

Pol. Fairly offer'd.

Cam. This shows a sound affection.

Shep. But, my daughter, 393
Say you the like to him?

Per. I cannot speak
So well, nothing so well; no, nor mean better:
By the pattern of mine own thoughts I cut out
The purity of his.

Shep. Take hands; a bargain; 396
And, friends unknown, you shall bear witness to 't:
I give my daughter to him, and will make
Her portion equal his.

Flo. O! that must be 399
I' the virtue of your daughter: one being dead,
I shall have more than you can dream of yet;
Enough then for your wonder. But, come on;
Contract us 'fore these witnesses.

Shep. Come, your hand;
And, daughter, yours.

Pol. Soft, swain, awhile, beseech you.
Have you a father?

Flo. I have; but what of him?

Pol. Knows he of this?

Flo. He neither does nor shall.

Pol. Methinks a father
Is, at the nuptial of his son, a guest 408
That best becomes the table. Pray you, once more,
Is not your father grown incapable
Of reasonable affairs? is he not stupid

391 perdition: *destruction*

Vith age and altering rheums? can he speak? hear? 412
:now man from man? dispute his own estate?
.ies he not bed-rid? and again does nothing
3ut what he did being childish?

Flo. No, good sir:
Ie has his health and ampler strength indeed
'han most have of his age.

Pol. By my white beard, 417
'ou offer him, if this be so, a wrong
omething unfilial. Reason my son
hould choose himself a wife, but as good reason 420
'he father,—all whose joy is nothing else
3ut fair posterity,—should hold some counsel
n such a business.

Flo. I yield all this;
3ut for some other reasons, my grave sir, 424
Vhich 'tis not fit you know, I not acquaint
Iy father of this business.

Pol. Let him know 't.

Flo. He shall not.

Pol. Prithee, let him.

Flo. No, he must not.

Shep. Let him, my son: he shall not need to grieve 428
t knowing of thy choice.

Flo. Come, come, he must not.
Iark our contract.

Pol. Mark your divorce, young sir,
[*Discovering himself.*]
Vhom son I dare not call: thou art too base
'o be acknowledg'd: thou a sceptre's heir, 432

12 rheums; *cf. n.*
13 dispute: *discuss* estate: *affairs* 419 Reason: *it is reasonable*

That thus affect'st a sheep-hook! Thou old traito
I am sorry that by hanging thee I can
But shorten thy life one week. And thou, fresh piec
Of excellent witchcraft, who of force must know
The royal fool thou cop'st with,—

Shep. O, my heart! 43

Pol. I'll have thy beauty scratch'd with briers, an
made
More homely than thy state. For thee, fond boy,
If I may ever know thou dost but sigh 44
That thou no more shalt see this knack,—as never
I mean thou shalt,—we'll bar thee from succession;
Not hold thee of our blood, no, not our kin,
Far than Deucalion off: mark thou my words:
Follow us to the court. Thou, churl, for thi
time, 44
Though full of our displeasure, yet we free thee
From the dead blow of it. And you, enchantment,–
Worthy enough a herdsman; yea, him too, 44
That makes himself, but for our honour therein,
Unworthy thee,—if ever henceforth thou
These rural latches to his entrance open,
Or hoop his body more with thy embraces, 45
I will devise a death as cruel for thee
As thou art tender to 't. *Exi*

Per. Even here undone!
I was not much afeard; for once or twice
I was about to speak and tell him plainly, 45
The self-same sun that shines upon his court
Hides not his visage from our cottage, but

433 affect'st: *aspirest to* 435 fresh: *youn*
436 of force: *of necessity* 437 cop'st: *deale*
439 state: *social position* fond: *foolish*
444 Far: *farther* Deucalion: *the Greek Noah*
445 churl: *peasant* 447 dead: *dead*

ooks on alike. Will 't please you, sir, be gone?
told you what would come of this: beseech you, 460
f your own state take care: this dream of mine—
eing now awake, I'll queen it no inch further,
ut milk my ewes and weep.

Cam. Why, how now, father!
peak, ere thou diest.

Shep. I cannot speak, nor think, 464
for dare to know that which I know. O sir!
'ou have undone a man of fourscore three,
'hat thought to fill his grave in quiet, yea,
'o die upon the bed my father died, 468
'o lie close by his honest bones: but now
ome hangman must put on my shroud and lay me
Vhere no priest shovels in dust. O cursed wretch!
'hat knew'st this was the prince, and wouldst adventure 472
'o mingle faith with him. Undone! undone!
f I might die within this hour, I have liv'd
'o die when I desire. *Exit.*

Flo. Why look you so upon me?
am but sorry, not afeard; delay'd, 476
But nothing alter'd. What I was, I am:
Iore straining on for plucking back; not following
Iy leash unwillingly.

Cam. Gracious my lord,
'ou know your father's temper: at this time 480
Ie will allow no speech, which I do guess
'ou do not purpose to him; and as hardly
Vill he endure your sight as yet, I fear:
Then, till the fury of his highness settle, 484
Come not before him.

73 mingle faith: *exchange troth-plights* 478 plucking: *being pulled*

Flo. I not purpose it.
I think, Camillo?
Cam. Even he, my lord.
Per. How often have I told you 'twould be thus!
How often said my dignity would last 48
But till 'twere known!
Flo. It cannot fail but by
The violation of my faith; and then
Let nature crush the sides o' the earth together
And mar the seeds within! Lift up thy looks:
From my succession wipe me, father; I 49
Am heir to my affection.
Cam. Be advis'd.
Flo. I am; and by my fancy: if my reason
Will thereto be obedient, I have reason; 49
If not, my senses, better pleas'd with madness,
Do bid it welcome.
Cam. This is desperate, sir.
Flo. So call it; but it does fulfil my vow;
I needs must think it honesty. Camillo, 50
Not for Bohemia, nor the pomp that may
Be thereat glean'd, for all the sun sees or
The close earth wombs or the profound sea hides
In unknown fathoms, will I break my oath 50
To this my fair belov'd. Therefore, I pray you,
As you have ever been my father's honour'd friend,
When he shall miss me,—as, in faith, I mean not
To see him any more,—cast your good counsels
Upon his passion: let myself and fortune 50
Tug for the time to come. This you may know
And so deliver, I am put to sea
With her whom here I cannot hold on shore;

494 Am heir to my affection: *have an inheritance in my love*
495 fancy: *love* 503 wombs: *bears within i*
510 Tug: *struggle (as in a tug-of-war)*

nd most opportune to our need, I have 513
vessel rides fast by, but not prepar'd
or this design. What course I mean to hold
hall nothing benefit your knowledge, nor 516
oncern me the reporting.

Cam. O my lord!
would your spirit were easier for advice,
r stronger for your need.

Flo. Hark, Perdita. [*Takes her aside.*]
To Camillo.] I'll hear you by and by.

Cam. He 's irremovable, 520
esolv'd for flight. Now were I happy if
is going I could frame to serve my turn,
ave him from danger, do him love and honour,
urchase the sight again of dear Sicilia 524
nd that unhappy king, my master, whom
so much thirst to see.

Flo. Now, good Camillo,
am so fraught with curious business that
leave out ceremony.

Cam. Sir, I think 528
ou have heard of my poor services, i' the love
'hat I have borne your father?

Flo. Very nobly
ave you deserv'd: it is my father's music
'o speak your deeds, not little of his care 532
'o have them recompens'd as thought on.

Cam. Well, my lord,
f you may please to think I love the king
nd through him what 's nearest to him, which is
our gracious self, embrace but my direction.
f your more ponderous and settled project 537

6 nor . . . reporting: *nor is it my business to tell you*
0 by and by: *in just a minute*
7 fraught: *loaded down* curious: *causing anxiety*

May suffer alteration, on mine honour
I'll point you where you shall have such receiving
As shall become your highness; where you may
Enjoy your mistress,—from the whom, I see, 54
There 's no disjunction to be made, but by,
As, heavens forfend! your ruin,—marry her;
And with my best endeavours in your absence
Your discontenting father strive to qualify, 54
And bring him up to liking.

Flo. How, Camillo,
May this, almost a miracle, be done?
That I may call thee something more than man,
And after that trust to thee.

Cam. Have you thought on 54
A place whereto you'll go?

Flo. Not any yet;
But as the unthought-on accident is guilty
To what we wildly do, so we profess 55
Ourselves to be the slaves of chance and flies
Of every wind that blows.

Cam. Then list to me:
This follows; if you will not change your purpose
But undergo this flight, make for Sicilia, 55
And there present yourself and your fair princess,—
For so, I see, she must be,—'fore Leontes;
She shall be habited as it becomes
The partner of your bed. Methinks I see 56
Leontes opening his free arms and weeping
His welcomes forth; asks thee, the son, forgiveness
As 'twere i' the father's person; kisses the hands
Of your fresh princess; o'er and o'er divides him 56

543 forfend: *forbid*
545 discontenting: *dissatisfied* qualify: *pacify*
546 bring him up to liking: *make him approve your choice*
551 guilty to: *to blame for* 564 him: *himse*

'wixt his unkindness and his kindness: the one
e chides to hell, and bids the other grow
aster than thought or time.

Flo. Worthy Camillo,
'hat colour for my visitation shall I 568
old up before him?

Cam. Sent by the king your father
o greet him and to give him comforts. Sir,
he manner of your bearing towards him, with
'hat you as from your father shall deliver, 572
hings known betwixt us three, I'll write you down:
he which shall point you forth at every sitting
'hat you must say; that he shall not perceive
ut that you have your father's bosom there 576
nd speak his very heart.

Flo. I am bound to you.
here is some sap in this.

Cam. A course more promising
han a wild dedication of yourselves
o unpath'd waters, undream'd shores, most certain 580
o miseries enough: no hope to help you,
ut as you shake off one to take another;
othing so certain as your anchors, who
o their best office, if they can but stay you 584
'here you'll be loath to be. Besides, you know
rosperity 's the very bond of love,
'hose fresh complexion and whose heart together
ffliction alters.

Per. One of these is true: 588
think affliction may subdue the cheek,
ut not take in the mind.

8 colour: *pretext*
4 point you forth: *direct you* sitting: *interview*
6 bosom: *inmost secrets* 578 sap: *juice, life* 590 take in: *conquer*

Cam. Yea, say you so?
There shall not at your father's house these seve
years
Be born another such.

Flo. My good Camillo, 59
She is as forward of her breeding as
She is i' the rear o' our birth.

Cam. I cannot say 'tis pity
She lacks instructions, for she seems a mistress
To most that teach.

Per. Your pardon, sir; for this 59
I'll blush you thanks.

Flo. My prettiest Perdita!
But O! the thorns we stand upon. Camillo,
Preserver of my father, now of me,
The med'cine of our house, how shall we do? 60
We are not furnish'd like Bohemia's son,
Nor shall appear in Sicilia.

Cam. My lord,
Fear none of this: I think you know my fortunes
Do all lie there: it shall be so my care 60
To have you royally appointed as if
The scene you play were mine. For instance, sir,
That you may know you shall not want, one word.
[*They talk aside*

Enter Autolycus.

Aut. Ha, ha! what a fool Honesty is! and Trust, his sworn brother, a very simple gentleman! I have sold all my trumpery: not a counterfeit stone, not a riband, glass, pomander,

593 forward of her breeding: *superior to her upbringing*
601 furnish'd: *equipped* 602 appear: *appear*
605 appointed: *fitted out* 611 pomander; *cf.*

brooch, table-book, ballad, knife, tape, glove, shoe-tie, bracelet, horn-ring, to keep my pack from fasting: they throng who should buy first, as if my trinkets had been hallowed and brought a benediction to the buyer: by which means 616 I saw whose purse was best in picture; and what I saw, to my good use I remembered. My clown,—who wants but something to be a reasonable man,—grew so in love with the wenches' song that he would not stir his pettitoes till he had both tune and words; which so drew the rest of the herd to me that all their other senses stuck in ears: you might have pinched a placket, it was senseless; 'twas nothing to geld a codpiece 625 of a purse; I would have filed keys off that hung in chains: no hearing, no feeling, but my sir's song, and admiring the nothing of it; so that, in this time of lethargy I picked and cut most of their festival purses; and had not the old man come in with a whoo-bub against his daughter and the king's son, and scared my choughs from the chaff, I had not left a purse alive in the whole army. 634

[*Camillo, Florizel, and Perdita come forward.*]

Cam. Nay, but my letters, by this means being there
So soon as you arrive, shall clear that doubt. 636

Flo. And those that you'll procure from King Leontes—

Cam. Shall satisfy your father.

Per. Happy be you!

612 table-book: *notebook*
617 picture: *appearance*
621 pettitoes: *pig's feet*
625 senseless: *insensible* geld a codpiece: *rob a breeches pocket*
631 whoo-bub: *outcry*
632 choughs: *jackdaws, simpletons*

All that you speak shows fair.

Cam. [*Seeing Autolycus.*] Whom have we here?
We'll make an instrument of this: omit 640
Nothing may give us aid.

Aut. [*Aside.*] If they have overheard me now, why, hanging.

Cam. How now, good fellow! Why shakest thou so? Fear not, man; here's no harm intended to thee.

Aut. I am a poor fellow, sir. 647

Cam. Why, be so still; here's nobody will steal that from thee; yet, for the outside of thy poverty we must make an exchange; therefore, discase thee instantly,—thou must think, there's a necessity in 't,—and change garments with this gentleman: though the pennyworth on his side be the worst, yet hold thee, there's some boot.

Aut. I am a poor fellow, sir.—[*Aside.*] I know ye well enough. 656

Cam. Nay, prithee, dispatch: the gentleman is half flayed already.

Aut. Are you in earnest, sir? [*Aside.*] I smell the trick on 't. 660

Flo. Dispatch, I prithee.

Aut. Indeed, I have had earnest; but I cannot with conscience take it.

Cam. Unbuckle, unbuckle.— 664

[*Florizel and Autolycus exchange garments.*]

Fortunate mistress,—let my prophecy
Come home to ye!—you must retire yourself
Into some covert: take your sweetheart's hat
And pluck it o'er your brows; muffle your face;

651 discase: *undress* 653 pennyworth: *bargain*
662 earnest: *part payment in advance*

Dismantle you, and, as you can, disliken 669
The truth of your own seeming; that you may,—
For I do fear eyes over you,—to shipboard
Get undescried.

Per. I see the play so lies 672
That I must bear a part.

Cam. No remedy.
Have you done there?

Flo. Should I now meet my father
He would not call me son.

Cam. Nay, you shall have no hat.
[*Giving it to Perdita.*]
Come, lady, come. Farewell, my friend.

Aut. Adieu, sir. 676

Flo. O Perdita, what have we twain forgot!
Pray you, a word. [*They converse apart.*]

Cam. [*Aside.*] What I do next shall be to tell the king
Of this escape, and whither they are bound; 680
Wherein my hope is I shall so prevail
To force him after: in whose company
I shall review Sicilia, for whose sight
I have a woman's longing.

Flo. Fortune speed us! 684
Thus we set on, Camillo, to the sea-side.

Cam. The swifter speed the better.
Exit [*with Florizel and Perdita*].

Aut. I understand the business; I hear it. To have an open ear, a quick eye, and a nimble hand, is necessary for a cut-purse: a good nose is requisite also, to smell out work for the other senses. I see this is the time that the unjust

669 Dismantle: *change your cloak* disliken: *disguise*
682 To: *as to* 683 review: *see again*

man doth thrive. What an exchange had this been without boot! what a boot is here with this exchange! Sure, the gods do this year connive 694 at us, and we may do anything extempore. The prince himself is about a piece of iniquity; stealing away from his father with his clog at his heels. If I thought it were a piece of honesty to acquaint the king withal, I would not do 't: I hold it the more knavery to conceal it, and therein am I constant to my profession. Aside, aside: here is more matter for a hot brain. Every lane's end, every shop, church, session, hanging, yields a careful man work. 704

Enter Clown and Shepherd.

Clo. See, see, what a man you are now! There is no other way but to tell the king she 's a changeling and none of your flesh and blood.

Shep. Nay, but hear me. 708

Clo. Nay, but hear me.

Shep. Go to, then.

Clo. She being none of your flesh and blood, your flesh and blood has not offended the king; and so your flesh and blood is not to be punished by him. Show those things you found about her; those secret things, all but what she has with her: this being done, let the law go whistle: I warrant you. 717

Shep. I will tell the king all, every word, yea, and his son's pranks too; who, I may say, is no honest man neither to his father nor to me, to go about to make me the king's brother-in-law. 722

699 withal: *therewith* 710 Go to: *go ahead*

Clo. Indeed, brother-in-law was the furthest off you could have been to him, and then your blood had been the dearer by I know not how much an ounce.

Aut. [*Aside.*] Very wisely, puppies! 727

Shep. Well, let us to the king: there is that in this fardel will make him scratch his beard.

Aut. [*Aside.*] I know not what impediment this complaint may be to the flight of my master. 732

Clo. Pray heartily he be at palace.

Aut. [*Aside.*] Though I am not naturally honest, I am so sometimes by chance: let me pocket up my pedlar's excrement. [*Takes off his false beard.*] How now, rustics! whither are you bound? 738

Shep. To the palace, an it like your worship. 740

Aut. Your affairs there, what, with whom, the condition of that fardel, the place of your dwelling, your names, your ages, of what having, breeding, and anything that is fitting to be known, discover. 745

Clo. We are but plain fellows, sir.

Aut. A lie; you are rough and hairy. Let me have no lying; it becomes none but tradesmen, and they often give us soldiers the lie; but we pay them for it with stamped coin, not stabbing steel; therefore they do not give us the lie. 752

Clo. Your worship had like to have given us

729 fardel: *bundle* 736 excrement: *excrescence, hair*
739 an: *if* like: *please* 743 having: *wealth*

one, if you had not taken yourself with the manner. 755

Shep. Are you a courtier, an 't like you, sir?

Aut. Whether it like me or no, I am a courtier. Seest thou not the air of the court in these enfoldings? hath not my gait in it the measure of the court? receives not thy nose court-odour from me? reflect I not on thy baseness court-contempt? Think'st thou, for that I 762 insinuate, or toaze from thee thy business, I am therefore no courtier? I am courtier, cap-a-pe, and one that will either push on or pluck back thy business there: whereupon I command thee to open thy affair.

Shep. My business, sir, is to the king. 768

Aut. What advocate hast thou to him?

Shep. I know not, an 't like you.

Clo. Advocate 's the court-word for a pheasant: say you have none. 772

Shep. None, sir; I have no pheasant, cock nor hen.

Aut. How bless'd are we that are not simple men!
Yet nature might have made me as these are,
Therefore I'll not disdain. 776

Clo. This cannot be but a great courtier.

Shep. His garments are rich, but he wears them not handsomely.

Clo. He seems to be the more noble in being fantastical: a great man, I'll warrant; I know by the picking on 's teeth.

Aut. The fardel there? what 's i' the fardel?
Wherefore that box? 784

754 with the manner: *in the act* 759 enfoldings: *garments*
760 measure: *stately tread*
763 insinuate: *wheedle* toaze: *draw out*
764 cap-a-pe: *from head to foot* 782 picking on's: *way he picks his*

Shep. Sir, there lies such secrets in this fardel and box which none must know but the king; and which he shall know within this hour if I may come to the speech of him. 788

Aut. Age, thou hast lost thy labour.

Shep. Why, sir?

Aut. The king is not at the palace; he is gone aboard a new ship to purge melancholy and air himself: for, if thou be'st capable of things serious, thou must know the king is full of grief.

Shep. So 'tis said, sir, about his son, that should have married a shepherd's daughter. 797

Aut. If that shepherd be not now in hand-fast, let him fly: the curses he shall have, the torture he shall feel, will break the back of man, the heart of monster. 801

Clo. Think you so, sir?

Aut. Not he alone shall suffer what wit can make heavy and vengeance bitter; but those that are germane to him, though removed fifty times, shall all come under the hangman: which though it be great pity, yet it is necessary. An 807 old sheep-whistling rogue, a ram-tender, to offer to have his daughter come into grace! Some say he shall be stoned; but that death is too soft for him, say I: draw our throne into a sheep cote! all deaths are too few, the sharpest too easy. 813

Clo. Has the old man e'er a son, sir, do you hear, an 't like you, sir?

Aut. He has a son, who shall be flayed alive; then 'nointed over with honey, set on the head

798 hand-fast: *custody* 805 germane: *related* 808 offer: *presume*

of a wasp's nest; then stand till he be three quarters and a dram dead; then recovered again with aqua-vitæ or some other hot infusion; then, raw as he is, and in the hottest day prognostication proclaims, shall he be set against a brick-wall, the sun looking with a southward eye upon him, where he is to behold him with flies blown 824 to death. But what talk we of these traitorly rascals, whose miseries are to be smiled at, their offences being so capital? Tell me,—for you seem to be honest plain men,—what you have to the king: being something gently considered, I'll bring you where he is aboard, tender your persons to his presence, whisper him in your behalfs; and if it be in man besides the king to effect your suits, here is a man shall do it. 833

Clo. He seems to be of great authority: close with him, give him gold; and though authority be a stubborn bear, yet he is oft led by the nose with gold. Show the inside of your purse to the outside of his hand, and no more ado. Remember, 'stoned,' and 'flayed alive'! 839

Shep. An 't please you, sir, to undertake the business for us, here is that gold I have: I'll make it as much more and leave this young man in pawn till I bring it you.

Aut. After I have done what I promised? 845

Shep. Ay, sir.

Aut. Well, give me the moiety. Are you a party in this business? 848

819 a dram: *a trifle more* 820 aqua-vitæ: *brandy*
821 prognostication: *the almanac's forecast of the weather*
825 what: *why*
829 considered: *given a consideration, bribed* 830 tender: *present*

Clo. In some sort, sir: but though my case be a pitiful one, I hope I shall not be flayed out of it.

Aut. O! that 's the case of the shepherd's son: hang him, he'll be made an example. 853

Clo. Comfort, good comfort! we must to the king and show our strange sights: he must know 'tis none of your daughter nor my sister; we are gone else. Sir, I will give you as much as this old man does when the business is performed; and remain, as he says, your pawn till it be brought you. 860

Aut. I will trust you. Walk before toward the sea-side; go on the right hand; I will but look upon the hedge and follow you.

Clo. We are blessed in this man, as I may say, even blessed. 865

Shep. Let 's before as he bids us. He was provided to do us good.

[*Exeunt Shepherd and Clown.*]

Aut. If I had a mind to be honest I see Fortune would not suffer me: she drops booties in my mouth. I am courted now with a double occasion, gold, and a means to do the prince my master good; which who knows how that may turn back to my advancement? I will 873 bring these two moles, these blind ones, aboard him: if he think it fit to shore them again, and that the complaint they have to the king concerns him nothing, let him call me rogue for being so far officious; for I am proof against that title and what shame else belongs to 't. To

849 case: *a pun on the two meanings, situation and skin*
874 aboard him: *aboard his ship* 875 shore: *put on shore*

him will I present them: there may be matter in it. *Exit.*

ACT FIFTH

Scene One

[*Sicilia. A Room in the Palace of Leontes*]

Enter Leontes, Cleomenes, Dion, Paulina, Servants.

Cleo. Sir, you have done enough, and have perform'd
A saint-like sorrow: no fault could you make
Which you have not redeem'd; indeed, paid down
More penitence than done trespass. At the last, 4
Do as the heavens have done, forget your evil;
With them forgive yourself.
Leon. Whilst I remember
Her and her virtues, I cannot forget
My blemishes in them, and so still think of 8
The wrong I did myself; which was so much,
That heirless it hath made my kingdom, and
Destroy'd the sweet'st companion that e'er man
Bred his hopes out of.
Paul. True, too true, my lord; 12
If one by one you wedded all the world,
Or from the all that are took something good,
To make a perfect woman, she you kill'd
Would be unparallel'd.
Leon. I think so. Kill'd! 16
She I kill'd! I did so; but thou strik'st me
Sorely to say I did: it is as bitter
Upon thy tongue as in my thought. Now, good now,
Say so but seldom.

19 good now: *pray you*

Cleo. Not at all, good lady: 20
You might have spoken a thousand things that would
Have done the time more benefit, and grac'd
Your kindness better.
Paul. You are one of those
Would have him wed again.
Dion. If you would not so, 24
You pity not the state, nor the remembrance
Of his most sovereign name; consider little
What dangers, by his highness' fail of issue,
May drop upon his kingdom and devour 28
Incertain lookers-on. What were more holy
Than to rejoice the former queen is well?
What holier than for royalty's repair,
For present comfort, and for future good, 32
To bless the bed of majesty again
With a sweet fellow to 't?
Paul. There is none worthy,
Respecting her that 's gone. Besides, the gods
Will have fulfil'd their secret purposes; 36
For has not the divine Apollo said,
Is 't not the tenour of his oracle,
That King Leontes shall not have an heir
Till his lost child be found? which that it shall,
Is all as monstrous to our human reason 41
As my Antigonus to break his grave
And come again to me; who, on my life,
Did perish with the infant. 'Tis your counsel 44
My lord should to the heavens be contrary,
Oppose against their wills.—[*To Leontes.*] Care not
for issue;
The crown will find an heir: great Alexander

22 done . . . benefit: *suited the occasion better* 27 fail: *lack*
29 Incertain: *irresolute*
31 repair: *restoration* 35 Respecting: *compared with*

Left his to the worthiest, so his successor 48
Was like to be the best.

Leon. Good Paulina,
Who hast the memory of Hermione,
I know, in honour; O! that ever I
Had squar'd me to thy counsel! then, even now, 52
I might have look'd upon my queen's full eyes,
Have taken treasure from her lips,—

Paul. And left them
More rich, for what they yielded.

Leon. Thou speak'st truth.
No more such wives; therefore, no wife: one worse, 56
And better us'd, would make her sainted spirit
Again possess her corpse and on this stage,—
Where we're offenders now,—appear soul-vex'd,
And begin, 'Why to me?'

Paul. Had she such power, 60
She had just cause.

Leon. She had; and would incense me
To murder her I married.

Paul. I should so:
Were I the ghost that walk'd, I'd bid you mark
Her eye, and tell me for what dull part in 't 64
You chose her; then I'd shriek, that even your ears
Should rift to hear me; and the words that follow'd
Should be 'Remember mine.'

Leon. Stars, stars!
And all eyes else dead coals. Fear thou no wife;
I'll have no wife, Paulina.

Paul. Will you swear 69
Never to marry but by my free leave?

52 squar'd me: *shaped my conduct*
61 incense: *incite*
66 rift: *rive, burst*

Leon. Never, Paulina: so be bless'd my spirit!
Paul. Then, good my lords, bear witness to his oath. 72
Cleo. You tempt him over much.
Paul. Unless another,
As like Hermione as is her picture,
Affront his eye.
Cleo. Good madam,—
Paul. I have done.
Yet, if my lord will marry,—if you will, sir, 76
No remedy, but you will,—give me the office
To choose you a queen, she shall not be so young
As was your former; but she shall be such
As, walk'd your first queen's ghost, it should take joy 80
To see her in your arms.
Leon. My true Paulina,
We shall not marry till thou bidd'st us.
Paul. That
Shall be when your first queen 's again in breath;
Never till then. 84

Enter a Servant.

Ser. One that gives out himself Prince Florizel,
Son of Polixenes, with his princess,—she
The fairest I have yet beheld,—desires access
To your high presence.
Leon. What with him? he comes not 88
Like to his father's greatness; his approach,
So out of circumstance and sudden, tells us
'Tis not a visitation fram'd, but forc'd
By need and accident. What train?

75 Affront: *confront* 84 S. d. Servant: *gentleman-in-waiting*
90 out of circumstance: *lacking in ceremony*
91 fram'd: *planned in advance*

Ser. But few, 92
And those but mean.

Leon. His princess, say you, with him?

Ser. Ay, the most peerless piece of earth, I think,
That e'er the sun shone bright on.

Paul. O Hermione!
As every present time doth boast itself 96
Above a better gone, so must thy grave
Give way to what 's seen now. Sir, you yourself
Have said and writ so,—but your writing now
Is colder than that theme,—'She had not been,
Nor was not to be equall'd'; thus your verse 101
Flow'd with her beauty once: 'tis shrewdly ebb'd
To say you have seen a better.

Ser. Pardon, madam:
The one I have almost forgot—your pardon—
The other, when she has obtain'd your eye, 105
Will have your tongue too. This is a creature,
Would she begin a sect, might quench the zeal
Of all professors else, make proselytes 108
Of who she but bid follow.

Paul. How! not women?

Ser. Women will love her, that she is a woman
More worth than any man; men, that she is
The rarest of all women.

Leon. Go, Cleomenes; 112
Yourself, assisted with your honour'd friends,
Bring them to our embracement. Still 'tis strange,
Exit [*Cleomenes with others*].
He thus should steal upon us.

Paul. Had our prince—
Jewel of children—seen this hour, he had pair'd

102 shrewdly: *exceedingly*
108 professors else: *those who profess other faiths* 113 with: *by*

Well with this lord: there was not full a month
Between their births.
  Leon. Prithee, no more: cease! thou know'st
He dies to me again when talk'd of: sure, 120
When I shall see this gentleman, thy speeches
Will bring me to consider that which may
Unfurnish me of reason. They are come.

Enter Florizel, Perdita, Cleomenes, and others.

Your mother was most true to wedlock, prince;
For she did print your royal father off, 125
Conceiving you. Were I but twenty-one,
Your father's image is so hit in you,
His very air, that I should call you brother, 128
As I did him; and speak of something wildly
By us perform'd before. Most dearly welcome!
And you, fair princess,—goddess! O, alas!
I lost a couple, that 'twixt heaven and earth 132
Might thus have stood begetting wonder as
You, gracious couple, do: and then I lost—
All mine own folly—the society,
Amity too, of your brave father, whom, 136
Though bearing misery, I desire my life
Once more to look on him.
  Flo. By his command
Have I here touch'd Sicilia; and from him
Give you all greetings that a king, at friend, 140
Can send his brother: and, but infirmity,—
Which waits upon worn times,—hath something seiz'd
His wish'd ability, he had himself
The land and waters 'twixt your throne and his
Measur'd to look upon you, whom he loves— 145

123 Unfurnish: *deprive*
140 at friend: *on friendly terms* 141-143 but . . . ability; *cf. n.*

He bade me say so—more than all the sceptres
And those that bear them living.

Leon. O, my brother!—
Good gentleman,—the wrongs I have done thee
stir 148
Afresh within me, and these thy offices
So rarely kind, are as interpreters
Of my behind-hand slackness! Welcome hither,
As is the spring to the earth. And hath he too
Expos'd this paragon to the fearful usage— 153
At least ungentle—of the dreadful Neptune,
To greet a man not worth her pains, much less
The adventure of her person?

Flo. Good my lord, 156
She came from Libya.

Leon. Where the warlike Smalus,
That noble honour'd lord, is fear'd and lov'd?

Flo. Most royal sir, from thence; from him, whose
daughter
His tears proclaim'd his, parting with her:
thence— 160
A prosperous south-wind friendly—we have cross'd,
To execute the charge my father gave me
For visiting your highness: my best train
I have from your Sicilian shores dismiss'd; 164
Who for Bohemia bend, to signify
Not only my success in Libya, sir,
But my arrival and my wife's, in safety
Here where we are.

Leon. The blessed gods 168
Purge all infection from our air whilst you
Do climate here! You have a holy father,

149 offices: *dutiful acts*
156 adventure: *risk*
165 bend: *steer*
170 climate: *reside*

A graceful gentleman; against whose person,
So sacred as it is, I have done sin: 172
For which the heavens, taking angry note,
Have left me issueless; and your father 's bless'd—
As he from heaven merits it—with you,
Worthy his goodness. What might I have been,
Might I a son and daughter now have look'd on,
Such goodly things as you!

Enter a Lord.

Lord. Most noble sir,
That which I shall report will bear no credit,
Were not the proof so nigh. Please you, great sir, 180
Bohemia greets you from himself by me;
Desires you to attach his son, who has—
His dignity and duty both cast off—
Fled from his father, from his hopes, and with
A shepherd's daughter.

Leon. Where 's Bohemia? speak. 185

Lord. Here in your city; I now came from him:
I speak amazedly, and it becomes
My marvel and my message. To your court 188
Whiles he was hastening,—in the chase it seems
Of this fair couple,—meets he on the way
The father of this seeming lady and
Her brother, having both their country quitted
With this young prince.

Flo. Camillo has betray'd me; 193
Whose honour and whose honesty till now
Endur'd all weathers.

171 graceful: *full of gracious qualities* 182 attach: *arrest*
187 amazedly: *in a maze* becomes: *befits*
188 marvel: *astonishment*

Lord. Lay 't so to his charge:
He 's with the king your father.
Leon. Who? Camillo? 196
Lord. Camillo, sir: I spake with him, who now
Has these poor men in question. Never saw I
Wretches so quake: they kneel, they kiss the earth,
Forswear themselves as often as they speak: 200
Bohemia stops his ears, and threatens them
With divers deaths in death.
Per. O my poor father!
The heaven sets spies upon us, will not have
Our contract celebrated.
Leon. You are married? 204
Flo. We are not, sir, nor are we like to be;
The stars, I see, will kiss the valleys first:
The odds for high and low 's alike.
Leon. My lord,
Is this the daughter of a king?
Flo. She is, 208
When once she is my wife.
Leon. That 'once,' I see, by your good father's speed,
Will come on very slowly. I am sorry,
Most sorry, you have broken from his liking 212
Where you were tied in duty; and as sorry
Your choice is not so rich in worth as beauty,
That you might well enjoy her.
Flo. Dear, look up:
Though Fortune, visible an enemy, 216
Should chase us with my father, power no jot
Hath she to change our loves. Beseech you, sir,
Remember since you ow'd no more to time
Than I do now; with thought of such affections,

207 *Cf. n.* 214 worth: *wealth and rank* 219 since: *when*

Step forth mine advocate; at your request 221
My father will grant precious things as trifles.

Leon. Would he do so, I'd beg your precious mistress,
Which he counts but a trifle.

Paul. Sir, my liege, 224
Your eye hath too much youth in 't: not a month
'Fore your queen died, she was more worth such gazes
Than what you look on now.

Leon. I thought of her,
Even in these looks I made. [*To Florizel.*] But your petition 228
Is yet unanswer'd. I will to your father:
Your honour not o'erthrown by your desires,
I am friend to them and you; upon which errand
I now go toward him. Therefore follow me, 232
And mark what way I make: come, good my lord.

Exeunt.

Scene Two

[*Before the Palace*]

Enter Autolycus and a Gentleman.

Aut. Beseech you, sir, were you present at this relation?

Gent. I was by at the opening of the fardel, heard the old shepherd deliver the manner how he found it: whereupon, after a little amazedness, we were all commanded out of the chamber; only this methought I heard the shepherd say, he found the child. 8

Aut. I would most gladly know the issue of it.

Gent. I make a broken delivery of the busi-

230 Your honour not: *provided your honor be not* 233 way: *progress*

ness; but the changes I perceived in the king and Camillo were very notes of admiration: they seemed almost, with staring on one another, to 13 tear the cases of their eyes; there was speech in their dumbness, language in their very gesture; they looked as they had heard of a world ransomed, or one destroyed: a notable passion of wonder appeared in them; but the wisest beholder, that knew no more but seeing, could not say if the importance were joy or sorrow; but in the extremity of the one it must needs be. 21

Enter another Gentleman.

Here comes a gentleman that haply knows more. The news, Rogero?

Sec. Gent. Nothing but bonfires: the oracle is fulfilled; the king's daughter is found: such a deal of wonder is broken out within this hour that ballad-makers cannot be able to express it.

Enter another Gentleman.

Here comes the lady Paulina's steward: he can deliver you more. How goes it now, sir? this news which is called true is so like an old tale, that the verity of it is in strong suspicion: has the king found his heir? 32

Third Gent. Most true, if ever truth were pregnant by circumstance: that which you hear you'll swear you see, there is such unity in the proofs. The mantle of Queen Hermione, her jewel about the neck of it, the letters of Anti-

12 notes: *distinctive marks* admiration: *wonder* 14 cases: *sockets*
20 importance: *import* in . . . one: *one in the highest degree*
34 pregnant by circumstance: *made full and convincing by circumstantial detail*
37 jewel: *jeweled necklace or similar ornament*

gonus found with it, which they know to be his character; the majesty of the creature in resemblance of the mother, the affection of nobleness which nature shows above her breeding, and many other evidences proclaim her with all certainty to be the king's daughter. Did you see the meeting of the two kings? 44

Sec. Gent. No.

Third Gent. Then have you lost a sight, which was to be seen, cannot be spoken of. There might you have beheld one joy crown another, so, and in such manner that, it seemed, sorrow wept to take leave of them, for their joy waded in tears. There was casting up of eyes, holding up of hands, with countenances of such distraction that they were to be known by garment, not by favour. Our king, being ready to leap out 54 of himself for joy of his found daughter, as if that joy were now become a loss, cries, 'O, thy mother, thy mother!' then asks Bohemia forgiveness; then embraces his son-in-law; then again worries he his daughter with clipping her; now he thanks the old shepherd, which stands by like a weather-bitten conduit of many kings' reigns. I never heard of such another encounter, which lames report to follow it and undoes description to do it. 64

Sec. Gent. What, pray you, became of Antigonus that carried hence the child?

Third Gent. Like an old tale still, which will have matter to rehearse, though credit be asleep and not an ear open. He was torn to pieces with

9 character: *handwriting*
40 affection of: *inclination toward*
4 favour: *face*
59 clipping: *embracing*
1 weather-bitten: *weather-worn; cf. n.*
64 do: *describe*

a bear: this avouches the shepherd's son, who has not only his innocence—which seems much —to justify him, but a handkerchief and rings of his that Paulina knows. 7

First Gent. What became of his bark and his followers?

Third Gent. Wrecked, the same instant of their master's death, and in the view of the shepherd: so that all the instruments which aided to expose the child were even then lost when it was found. But, O! the noble combat that 'twixt joy and sorrow was fought in Paulina. She had one eye declined for the loss of her husband, another elevated that the oracle was fulfilled: she lifted the princess from the earth, and so locks her in embracing, as if she would pin her to her heart that she might no more be in danger of losing. 8

First Gent. The dignity of this act was worth the audience of kings and princes, for by such was it acted.

Third Gent. One of the prettiest touches of all, and that which angled for mine eyes,—caught the water though not the fish,—was when at the relation of the queen's death, with the manner how she came to it,—bravely confessed and lamented by the king,—how attentiveness wounded his daughter; till, from one sign of dolour to another, she did, with an 'alas!' I would fain say, bleed tears, for I am sure my 9 heart wept blood. Who was most marble there changed colour; some swounded, all sorrowed:

71 innocence: *stupidity*
72 justify: *confirm*
100 marble: *i.e., stony-hearted*
101 swounded: *swooned*

if all the world could have seen 't, the woe had been universal. 103

First Gent. Are they returned to the court?

Third Gent. No; the princess hearing of her mother's statue, which is in the keeping of Paulina—a piece many years in doing, and now newly performed by that rare Italian master, Julio Romano; who, had he himself eternity 109 and could put breath into his work, would beguile Nature of her custom, so perfectly he is her ape: he so near to Hermione hath done Hermione that they say one would speak to her and stand in hope of answer: thither with all greediness of affection are they gone, and there they intend to sup. 116

Sec. Gent. I thought she had some great matter there in hand, for she hath privately, twice or thrice a day, ever since the death of Hermione, visited that removed house. Shall we thither and with our company piece the rejoicing? 122

First Gent. Who would be thence that has the benefit of access? every wink of an eye some new grace will be born: our absence makes us unthrifty to our knowledge. Let 's along. 126

Exeunt [*Gentlemen*].

Aut. Now, had I not the dash of my former life in me, would preferment drop on my head. I brought the old man and his son aboard the prince; told him I heard them talk of a fardel

109 Julio Romano; *cf. n.* eternity: *immortality*
111 custom: *customers, trade*
112 ape: *imitator*
120 removed: *distant*
121 piece: *add to*
124 access: *privilege of admittance*
126 unthrifty to: *careless about the increase of*

and I know not what; but he at that time, over-fond of the shepherd's daughter,—so he then took her to be,—who began to be much sea-sick, and himself little better, extremity of weather continuing, this mystery remained undiscovered. But 'tis all one to me; for had I been the finder out of this secret, it would not have relished among my other discredits. Here come those I have done good to against my will, and already appearing in the blossoms of their fortune. 141

Enter Shepherd and Clown.

Shep. Come, boy; I am past moe children, but thy sons and daughters will be all gentlemen born. 144

Clo. You are well met, sir. You denied to fight with me this other day, because I was no gentleman born: see you these clothes? say you see them not and think me still no gentleman born: you were best say these robes are not gentleman born. Give me the lie, do, and try whether I am not now a gentleman born.

Aut. I know you are now, sir, a gentleman born. 153

Clo. Ay, and have been so any time these four hours.

Shep. And so have I, boy. 156

Clo. So you have: but I was a gentleman born before my father; for the king's son took me by the hand and called me brother; and then the two kings called my father brother; and then the prince my brother and the princess

137 relished: *tasted well, been pleasing* 145 denied: *refused*

my sister called my father father; and so we wept: and there was the first gentleman-like tears that ever we shed. 164

Shep. We may live, son, to shed many more.

Clo. Ay; or else 'twere hard luck, being in so preposterous estate as we are.

Aut. I humbly beseech you, sir, to pardon me all the faults I have committed to your worship, and to give me your good report to the prince my master.

Shep. Prithee, son, do; for we must be gentle, now we are gentlemen. 173

Clo. Thou wilt amend thy life?

Aut. Ay, an it like your good worship.

Clo. Give me thy hand: I will swear to the prince thou art as honest a true fellow as any is in Bohemia. 178

Shep. You may say it, but not swear it.

Clo. Not swear it, now I am a gentleman? Let boors and franklins say it, I'll swear it.

Shep. How if it be false, son? 182

Clo. If it be ne'er so false, a true gentleman may swear it in the behalf of his friend: and I'll swear to the prince thou art a tall fellow of thy hands and that thou wilt not be drunk; but I know thou art no tall fellow of thy hands and that thou wilt be drunk: but I'll swear it, and I would thou wouldst be a tall fellow of thy hands.

Aut. I will prove so, sir, to my power. 191

Clo. Ay, by any means prove a tall fellow: if I do not wonder how thou darest venture to

167 preposterous: *blunder for prosperous*
181 franklins: *small landholders*
185 tall: *bold*

be drunk, not being a tall fellow, trust me not.
Hark! the kings and the princes, our kindred,
are going to see the queen's picture. Come,
follow us: we'll be thy good masters. 197

Exeunt.

Scene Three

[*A Chapel in Paulina's House*]

Enter Leontes, Polixenes, Florizel, Perdita, Camillo, Paulina, Lords, and Attendants.

Leon. O grave and good Paulina, the great comfort
That I have had of thee!

Paul. What, sovereign sir,
I did not well, I meant well. All my services
You have paid home; but that you have vouchsaf'd, 4
With your crown'd brother and these your contracted
Heirs of your kingdoms, my poor house to visit,
It is a surplus of your grace, which never
My life may last to answer.

Leon. O Paulina! 8
We honour you with trouble: but we came
To see the statue of our queen: your gallery
Have we pass'd through, not without much content
In many singularities, but we saw not 12
That which my daughter came to look upon,
The statue of her mother.

Paul. As she liv'd peerless,
So her dead likeness, I do well believe,
Excels whatever yet you look'd upon 16

196 picture: *painted statue* 197 good masters: *patrons*
9 We honour you with trouble: *our so-called honor but makes you trouble*
11 content: *pleasure* 12 singularities: *curiosities*

Or hand of man hath done; therefore I keep it
Lonely, apart. But here it is: prepare
To see the life as lively mock'd as ever
Still sleep mock'd death: behold! and say 'tis
well. 20

[*Paulina draws back a curtain, and reveals Hermione as a statue.*]

I like your silence: it the more shows off
Your wonder; but yet speak: first you, my liege.
Comes it not something near?

Leon. Her natural posture!
Chide me, dear stone, that I may say, indeed 24
Thou art Hermione; or rather, thou art she
In thy not chiding, for she was as tender
As infancy and grace. But yet, Paulina,
Hermione was not so much wrinkled; nothing
So aged as this seems.

Pol. O! not by much. 29

Paul. So much the more our carver's excellence;
Which lets go by some sixteen years and makes her
As she liv'd now.

Leon. As now she might have done, 32
So much to my good comfort, as it is
Now piercing to my soul. O! thus she stood,
Even with such life of majesty,—warm life,
As now it coldly stands,—when first I woo'd her.
I am asham'd: does not the stone rebuke me 37
For being more stone than it? O, royal piece!
There 's magic in thy majesty, which has
My evils conjur'd to remembrance, and 40
From thy admiring daughter took the spirits,
Standing like stone with thee.

19 lively: *to the life* 28 nothing: *not nearly* 38 piece: *woman*

Per. And give me leave,
And do not say 'tis superstition, that
I kneel and then implore her blessing. Lady, 44
Dear queen, that ended when I but began,
Give me that hand of yours to kiss.

Paul. O, patience!
The statue is but newly fix'd, the colour 's
Not dry. 48

Cam. My lord, your sorrow was too sore laid on,
Which sixteen winters cannot blow away,
So many summers dry: scarce any joy
Did ever so long live; no sorrow 52
But kill'd itself much sooner.

Pol. Dear my brother,
Let him that was the cause of this have power
To take off so much grief from you as he
Will piece up in himself.

Paul. Indeed, my lord, 56
If I had thought the sight of my poor image
Would thus have wrought you,--for the stone is mine,—
I'd not have show'd it.

Leon. Do not draw the curtain.

Paul. No longer shall you gaze on 't, lest your fancy 60
May think anon it moves.

Leon. Let be, let be!
Would I were dead, but that, methinks, already—
What was he that did make it? See, my lord,
Would you not deem it breath'd, and that those veins 64
Did verily bear blood?

56 piece up in himself: *make up by increasing his own grief*
58 wrought: *excited*

Pol. Masterly done:
The very life seems warm upon her lip.
Leon. The fixure of her eye has motion in 't,
As we are mock'd with art.
Paul. I'll draw the curtain; 68
My lord 's almost so far transported that
He'll think anon it lives.
Leon. O sweet Paulina!
Make me to think so twenty years together:
No settled senses of the world can match 72
The pleasure of that madness. Let 't alone.
Paul. I am sorry, sir, I have thus far stirr'd you: but
I could afflict you further.
Leon. Do, Paulina;
For this affliction has a taste as sweet 76
As any cordial comfort. Still, methinks,
There is an air comes from her: what fine chisel
Could ever yet cut breath? Let no man mock me,
For I will kiss her.
Paul. Good my lord, forbear. 80
The ruddiness upon her lip is wet:
You'll mar it if you kiss it; stain your own
With oily painting. Shall I draw the curtain?
Leon. No, not these twenty years.
Per. So long could I 84
Stand by, a looker-on.
Paul. Either forbear,
Quit presently the chapel, or resolve you
For more amazement. If you can behold it,
I'll make the statue move indeed, descend, 88
And take you by the hand; but then you'll think,—

67 *Cf. n.* 77 cordial: *restorative*
86 resolve you: *prepare yourselves*

Which I protest against,—I am assisted
By wicked powers

Leon. What you can make her do,
I am content to look on: what to speak, 92
I am content to hear; for 'tis as easy
To make her speak as move.

Paul. It is requir'd
You do awake your faith. Then, all stand still;
Or those that think it is unlawful business 96
I am about, let them depart.

Leon. Proceed:
No foot shall stir.

Paul. Music, awake her: strike! [*Music.*]
'Tis time; descend; be stone no more: approach;
Strike all that look upon with marvel. Come;
I'll fill your grave up: stir; nay, come away; 101
Bequeath to death your numbness, for from him
Dear life redeems you. You perceive she stirs:
[*Hermione comes down.*]
Start not; her actions shall be holy as 104
You hear my spell is lawful: do not shun her
Until you see her die again, for then
You kill her double. Nay, present your hand:
When she was young you woo'd her; now in age 108
Is she become the suitor!

Leon. [*Embracing her.*] O! she 's warm.
If this be magic, let it be an art
Lawful as eating.

Pol. She embraces him.

Cam. She hangs about his neck: 112
If she pertain to life let her speak too.

Pol. Ay; and make 't manifest where she has liv'd,
Or how stol'n from the dead.

100 upon: *on* 107 double: *doubly, twice*

Paul. That she is living,
Were it but told you, should be hooted at 116
Like an old tale; but it appears she lives,
Though yet she speak not. Mark a little while.
Please you to interpose, fair madam: kneel
And pray your mother's blessing. Turn, good lady; 120
Our Perdita is found.

[*Presenting Perdita, who kneels to Hermione.*]

Her. You gods, look down,
And from your sacred vials pour your graces
Upon my daughter's head! Tell me, mine own,
Where hast thou been preserv'd? where liv'd? how found 124
Thy father's court? for thou shalt hear that I,
Knowing by Paulina that the oracle
Gave hope thou wast in being, have preserv'd
Myself to see the issue.

Paul. There 's time enough for that; 128
Lest they desire upon this push to trouble
Your joys with like relation. Go together,
You precious winners all: your exultation
Partake to every one. I, an old turtle, 132
Will wing me to some wither'd bough, and there
My mate, that 's never to be found again,
Lament till I am lost.

Leon. O! peace, Paulina.
Thou shouldst a husband take by my consent, 136
As I by thine a wife: this is a match,
And made between 's by vows. Thou hast found mine;
But how, is to be question'd; for I saw her,

129 push: *impulse* 130 relation: *relating of their adventures*
132 Partake to: *share with* 137 match: *bargain*

As I thought dead, and have in vain said many 140
A prayer upon her grave. I'll not seek far,—
For him, I partly know his mind,—to find thee
An honourable husband. Come, Camillo,
And take her by the hand; whose worth and honesty 144
Is richly noted, and here justified
By us, a pair of kings. Let 's from this place.
What! look upon my brother: both your pardons,
That e'er I put between your holy looks 148
My ill suspicion. This' your son-in-law,
And son unto the king,—whom heavens directing,
Is troth-plight to your daughter. Good Paulina,
Lead us from hence, where we may leisurely 152
Each one demand and answer to his part
Perform'd in this wide gap of time since first
We were dissever'd: hastily lead away. *Exeunt.*

145 richly noted: *thoroughly known* justified: *vouched for*
149 This': *this is*

FINIS.

NOTES

Dramatis Personæ. This play is one of seven for which, under the caption 'The Names of the Actors,' the First Folio lists the Dramatis Personæ. The words put in brackets are there omitted.

I. i. 9, 10. *entertainment . . . loves.* 'Our loving welcome shall atone for our inadequate entertainment.'

I. i. 34, 35. *from . . . winds.* 'From the opposite corners of the heavens,' where the winds of the north, east, south, and west were supposed to have their homes.

I. ii. 1. *the watery star.* The moon, as cause of the tides, was considered the queen of the waters.

I. ii. 6, 7. *like . . . place.* 'As a cipher, though worthless in itself, may, in a significant position change thousands into tens of thousands, so my grateful farewell, though wholly inadequate, increases all previous expressions of gratitude.'

I. ii. 12. *that may blow.* This is usually interpreted as a wish. 'May there blow no nipping winds.'

I. ii. 41. *gest.* The gests of a royal journey (from the old French *giste,* a bed or lodging) were the houses at which the monarch stopped overnight on his way.

I. ii. 48. *unsphere the stars with oaths.* 'Shake the stars from their positions in the heavens by the violence of your oaths.' According to the ancient Ptolemaic theory of astronomy the earth was the center of the universe, and the stars were located in concentric hollow spheres revolving around it.

I. ii. 53. *pay your fees.* It was formerly a custom in prisons for a jailer to exact fees from his prisoners.

I. ii. 74. *the imposition, etc.* 'Setting aside our hereditary taint of original sin.'

I. ii. 92. *one good deed, etc.* 'The failure to praise one good deed prevents the existence of a thousand that would have been inspired by it.'

I. ii. 120. *brows.* It was a common saying in Shakespeare's time that an unfaithful wife put horns on her husband's head, or brows. The unsavory joke appears repeatedly.

I. ii. 126. *virginalling.* Playing as on the keys of the virginal, an old-time instrument resembling a piano. The word is here, as often, used punningly.

I. ii. 139-144. *Affection . . . dost.* A possible interpretation of this much disputed passage is: 'Love, thy intense passion masters the inmost hearts of women. Thou dost make possible on their part sins not believed to be possible. Thou dost make absent lovers communicate with each other through dreams (how can this be?). Thou dost cause the dreaming woman to make love to the unreal dream-image of her absent paramour, and to embrace nothingness. Then it is very believable that thou mayst bring her to the arms of a lover bodily present; and thou dost.' For another interpretation cf. C. D. Stewart, *Some Textual Difficulties in Shakespeare* (Yale University Press), pp. 96-109.

I. ii. 202. *predominant.* Leontes accepts the theory of astrology that certain stars under the right conditions exercise a powerful influence over human conduct.

I. ii. 273-275. *If . . . thought.* 'If thou wilt confess the truth—and to do otherwise thou must be one who impudently denies his possession of eyes or ears or thought—then say that my wife is a loose woman.'

I. ii. 280. *clouded.* Shakespeare's language is so figurative that a sharp line cannot always be drawn between metaphors and obsolete meanings. In the present case, which is typical of hundreds, he probably thought of the accusation dimming Hermione's fair rep tion as a cloud dims the moon.

I. ii. 307. *medal.* Medallions with the portrait of

a friend or sweetheart were frequently worn around the neck in Shakespeare's day. Leontes' jealous delirium pictures Hermione with her arms around Polixenes' neck and her living face on his bosom where the medallion with her portrait might hang.

I. ii. 458-460. 'May good speed in escaping help me, and bring comfort to the gracious queen, who is part of the subject of his thoughts but in no way the intentional cause of his ill-founded suspicion.' The passage is blind, and may have been garbled in printing.

II. i. S. d. The Folio stage direction reads: 'Enter Hermione, Mamillius, Ladies: Leontes, Antigonus, Lords.' Editors have agreed in placing the entrance of Leontes after line 31. In the Folio text of *The Winter's Tale* stage directions repeatedly mention actors who were probably to be ready when thus mentioned, but who evidently did not appear before the audience until later. In the present edition such stage directions are adapted according to the judgment of later editors.

II. i. 40. *partake no venom.* The belief was formerly common that a spider in one's drink made the beverage poisonous if the insect was seen, but not if the insect was unobserved. 'In the cup of my family life,' says Leontes, 'there has been the spider of adultery; but it did not poison my mind with jealous suffering as long as I did not perceive it.'

II. i. 133, 134. *I'll . . . wife.* 'I'll consider human beings on a level with horses in morality.'

II. i. 142. *land-damn.* Nothing but guesses can be given for the meaning of *land-damn.* It may mean to bury alive under the ground (land), to exile from the land, or it may be equivalent to *landan,* the word for a rural punishment in Gloucestershire for slanderers and adulterers, 'by rustics traversing from house to house along the country side, blowing trumpets and beating drums or pans and kettles.'

II. i. 152. While saying this Leontes probably pulls Antigonus' beard or offers him some other minor physical violence.

II. i. 175-178. *Which . . . deed.* 'Which was as gross as was ever found by a suspicion (conjecture) that lacked sight [of their crime] only, lacked nought for proof (approbation), except actually seeing them in sin—with all other circumstances pointing (made up) to the deed—all these, etc.'

II. i. 182. *Delphos.* The famous oracle of Apollo was at Delphi (or Delphos). Its location was on the mainland, but it is spoken of at the beginning of Act Third as being on an 'isle,' probably because it has been confused with the island of Delos. The play bristles with inaccuracies in history and geography, which the author did not consider out of keeping with its romantic atmosphere, and most of which he merely took over from the novel that served him as his source. In the main the story seems located in the Middle Ages, whereas the oracle belongs to a much earlier pagan period.

II. iii. 38. *humour.* It was formerly the general belief that there were four liquids (humours) in the body and that diseases were due to a disproportionate amount of some one of them.

II. iii. 75. *dame Partlet.* Dame Pertelote (Partlet) was a curtain-lecturing hen in Chaucer's *Nun's Priest's Tale.*

III. ii. 60-62. *More . . . acknowledge.* 'I must not at all acknowledge that I am guilty (mistress) of anything more than [that] which is counted against me as a fault [namely, my innocent hospitality toward Polixenes].'

III. ii. 82. 'My life is exposed to the deadly aim (level) of your jealous imaginings.'

III. ii. 168. *Unclasp'd.* The meaning 'revealed,' like so many Shakespearean meanings, was probably more metaphorical than literal even in the author's day. In *King Henry IV, Part I* (I. iii. 188) Worcester begins his revelation to Hotspur:

'And now I will unclasp a secret book.'

III. iii. 47, 48. *Which . . . thine.* 'Which may, if fortune is willing, by their great value inspire people to educate (breed) thee, and still remain thy property.'

III. iii. 59. *ten.* Most modern editors put *sixteen* or *nineteen* in the place of *ten,* on the ground that so early an age does not harmonize with all the offences mentioned. But the author was representing an ignorant and excited man who did not choose his words with the calm precision of a Shakespearean commentator.

III. iii. 100. *flap-dragoned.* A flap-dragon was a raisin or some other substance floating in a glass of brandy, from which some gallant, wishing to show his dexterity, would snatch it with his mouth. The sea gulped down the ship with the easy dexterity with which a toper would gulp down the flap-dragon.

IV. iii. 4. *winter's pale.* 'Pale' with Shakespeare had two frequent and widely different meanings, (1) paleness, and (2) an enclosed space, either one of which here would make sense. Consequently we could interpret the line: 'The red blood of youth and spring reigns in the pale face of winter'; or, 'The red blood reigns in those fields which recently were the enclosed park of winter.'

IV. iii. 23. It was a common belief that kites stole small linen articles to use in building their nests. My trade, says Autolycus, is in stealing sheets. Look out for lesser linen when the kites are building, but for sheets when I come by.

IV. iii. 25. *littered under Mercury.* Born under the influence of the planet Mercury, he naturally imitated the god Mercury, who was the ancient deity of thieves.

IV. iii. 47. *puritan.* The puritans were hostile to

the stage and consequently attacked repeatedly by Shakespeare and his fellow dramatists. Their habit of singing psalms was only one of their many traits ridiculed.

IV. iv. 13. *swoon.* The original text reads *sworn,* and the emendation *swoon,* though now generally adopted, is not very well in harmony with Perdita's healthful life and courageous character. If Shakespeare wrote *sworn,* Perdita probably meant that Florizel had come with the vowed purpose of showing in his plain clothes the opposite of her rich ones, as printed letters in a looking-glass are shown reading backwards.

IV. iv. 27-30. Jupiter became a bull to win the love of Europa; Neptune, a ram when in love with Theophane; and Apollo as a humble shepherd kept the flocks of King Admetus.

IV. iv. 76. *Grace and remembrance.* These were symbolized by rue and rosemary respectively. The significance of flowers as emblems of human moods was often mentioned by the Elizabethans, and plays an important part in the mad speeches of Ophelia (*Hamlet,* IV. v.).

IV. iv. 87, 88. *There . . . nature.* Their variegated colors are partly the result of the gardener's art in cross-breeding, and not wholly produced by nature.

IV. iv. 104. Lavender, savory, and certain varieties of marjoram were flowers recently imported into England from southern Europe. It is probably as natives of a warmer climate that Perdita calls them 'hot' and a few lines later speaks of them as 'flowers of middle summer.'

IV. iv. 116. *Proserpina.* While Proserpina was gathering flowers in the meadows of Sicily, Dis, or Pluto, the god of the underworld, rose through the earth in his chariot, seized her, and carried her away to be his queen.

IV. iv. 134. *Whitsun pastorals.* A pastoral is a play of country life; and a Whitsun play would be one given at Whitsuntide, the seventh Sunday after Easter, although we have no evidence elsewhere that plays given then were pastorals.

IV. iv. 195, 196. Dildos, fadings, 'jump her and thump her' were all catch words from the anything but 'delicate' refrains of certain popular songs and ballads.

IV. iv. 252. *tawdry lace.* This necklace or necktie of silk derived its name from Saint Audrey (Ethelreda), who believed a tumor which came in her throat to be a divine judgment on her for her vanity earlier in wearing beautiful necklaces.

IV. iv. 412. *altering rheums.* Morbid disarrangement of the four humours (see note on II. iii. 38), a condition producing rheumatism, catarrh, and the diseases characteristic of old age.

IV. iv. 611. *pomander.* A little ball of perfumes worn in the pocket or about the neck as a preventive against the plague.

V. i. 141-143. 'But that the infirmity which comes with age has somewhat stolen from him (seized) the traveling ability which he wishes for.'

V. i. 207. Probably, 'the odds are as great against me in my princely rôle of Florizel as they were in my humble rôle of Doricles.'

V. ii. 61. Conduits were often in the shape of human figures.

V. ii. 109. *Julio Romano.* This Italian painter was born in 1492, the year of America's discovery; and the worship of Apollo's oracle ceased among Mediterranean kings about a thousand years before that. Both Shakespeare and his audience had a sublime indifference to such anachronisms in a well-told story.

V. iii. 67. 'Though her eye be fixed, yet it seems to have motion in it.' (Edwards.)

APPENDIX A

Sources of the Play

The Winter's Tale is an excellent example of a novel turned into a play. That practice was common in Elizabethan times as in recent years; but with this difference, that the drama in Shakespeare's time was usually an improvement on the novel and in our own day is usually a popularized degradation of the original. The novel—or novelette, for it can be read in an hour—from which Shakespeare drew most of the plot of his *Winter's Tale* was *Pandosto: the Triumph of Time* (or *The Historie of Dorastus and Fawnia*), which first appeared in 1588 and was a 'best-seller' for years before Shakespeare dramatized it. At least fourteen editions of it are known to have been issued. Its author was Robert Greene, a brilliant and unfortunate author, who died near the beginning of Shakespeare's career, and died bitterly jealous of that transforming genius which was already giving hints of the masterpieces it could make from other men's crude materials.

In Greene's novel Pandosto, king of Bohemia, with his wife Bellaria entertains as his guest his old friend Egistus, king of Sicilia. Pandosto, like Leontes, becomes jealous, but more slowly and with more reason, for Bellaria, though pure, is imprudent. Franion, his cup-bearer, promises murder and escapes, as does Camillo. Bellaria, like Hermione, is accused. cleared by the oracle, and actually—not apparently—dies on learning the death of her son Garinter. Her little daughter Fawnia is abandoned on the coast of Sicilia, brought up by a shepherd, and loved by Prince Dorastus of that country. Capnio, a faithful old servant of Dorastus, aids the young lovers in their flight, as does Camillo, and brings the shepherd and 'fardel' aboard Dorastus' ship as does Shakespeare's Autolycus. The reception of the lovers at the court of Pandosto and the discovery of Fawnia's identity run closely parallel to the same events in the play, save that Pandosto, before learning Fawnia's parentage, conceives an incestuous love for his own daughter. After Fawnia's marriage Pandosto, grown melancholy with brooding over his sins against those whom he loved best, kills himself.

Shakespeare in recasting Greene's material omitted as too tragic and brutal the incestuous passion and violent death of Pandosto, and threw out as impertinent several paragraphs dealing with the life of the old shepherd. He created the characters of Antigonus, Paulina, and Autolycus, and combined the parts of Franion and Capnio in that of Camillo. He created the statue scene which ends the play, and the scene between Perdita and Polixenes (IV. iv.), for which there were no hints in the prose tale. By interchanging throughout the parts of Bohemia and Sicily he probably meant to veil the extent of his debt to a book that was still popular, although he may have believed that the suddenness of Leontes' jealousy would seem truer to life in a hot-blooded Sicilian than in a native of Central Europe. As is almost inevitable when changing a novel into a play, the action is made more rapid. For example, in the second scene of Act First events which in Greene's novel covered several weeks are made to happen in a single hour. The greatest change, however, and the greatest improvement, is in the conception of character, which throughout is more noble and subtle in Shakespeare than in his forerunner.

The closeness of Shakespeare at times to his original can be shown by comparing Hermione's defence (III. ii. 23-117) with the corresponding speech of Bellaria:

'If the deuine powers bee priuy to humane actions (as no doubt they are) I hope my patience shall make fortune blushe, and my vnspotted life shall staine spightfully discredit. For although lying Report hath sought to appeach mine honor, and Suspition hath intended to soyle my credit with infamie: yet where Vertue keepeth the Forte, Report and suspition may assayle, but neuer sack: how I haue led my life before Egistus comming, I appeale Pandosto to the Gods & to thy conscience. What hath passed betwixt him and me, the Gods onely know, and I hope will presently reueale: that I loued Egistus I can not denie: that I honored him I shame not to confesse: to the one I was forced by his vertues, to the other for his dignities. But as touching lasciuious lust, I say Egistus is honest, and hope my selfe to be found without spot: for Franion, I can neither accuse him nor excuse him, for I was not priuie to his departure, and that this is true which I haue heere rehearsed, I referre myselfe to the deuine Oracle.' [ed. Grosart, 4. 260.]

Vague likenesses between *The Winter's Tale* and certain other books have been pointed out; but none are close enough to prove borrowing on Shakespeare's part.

APPENDIX B

The History of the Play

The Winter's Tale was first 'allowed of,' or officially approved for performance, by Sir George Buck, who assumed office as Master of the Revels in 1610; consequently, although Buck did license plays before taking office, we may reasonably assume that it was not written previous to that year. Yet it was already on the stage by May 15, 1611, for a Dr. Simon Forman saw it acted on that date and has left a written record of the fact with an analysis of the plot. The dance of twelve satyrs in IV. iv. was probably suggested by a similar dance of satyrs in Ben Jonson's *Masque of Oberon,* first acted on the opening day of January, 1611. It seems practically certain, therefore, that the play was finished and first staged in the spring of 1611. It was for several years following a favorite at court, and in 1613 was acted with several other Shakespearean dramas before the Prince Palatine and his bride. No Quarto editions of it exist; apparently it first appeared in print in the Folio of 1623.

After Shakespeare's death the play, despite its beauty, was unpopular and almost unnoticed for over a century, more so than many of the author's other works. Certain fantastic qualities in it—the seacoast of Bohemia, a country which for centuries had no seacoast, and the sixteen-year interval between the third and fourth acts—jarred on the new age, an age which was more fastidious in such matters than the imaginative Elizabethans had been.

In 1741, however, *The Winter's Tale*—'not acted 100 years,' according to the historian Genest—was revived at Goodman's Fields, and the following year at the more famous theatre of Covent Garden. Soon afterward several adaptations of parts of it were made, the most notable being that of the great actor David Garrick (1717-1779), which was played at Drury Lane theatre in 1756. The play in Garrick's adaptation begins with what was Shakespeare's fourth act. The events of sixteen years earlier are rehearsed for the benefit of the audience in a conversation between Camillo and a gentleman. Then the repentant Leontes comes to Bohemia, takes part with Polixenes and Perdita in the conversation at the shepherd's feast, and assumes the part which Shakespeare gave Camillo of comforting the lovers. Florizel and Perdita do not take ship; and the closing statue scene is in Bohemia. Garrick's version was popular for more than a generation. The prosaic ingenuity with which he dovetailed together parts of Shakespeare's great work is well illustrated in the following passage:

Perd. One of these is true,
I think affliction may subdue the cheek,
But not take in the mind.

Leon. Yea, say you so?
There shall not at your father's house, these sev'n years,
Be born another such.

Flor. O reverend, Sir!
As you would wish a child of your own youth
To meet his happiness in love, speak for me;
Remember since you ow'd no more to time
Than I do now; and with thought of like affections,
Step forth my advocate.

Leon. You touch me deep,
Deep, to the quick, sweet prince; alas! alas!
I lost a daughter, that 'twixt heaven and earth
Might thus have stood begetting wonder, as
Yon lovely maiden does—of that no more;—
I'll to the king your father,—this our compact,
Your honour not o'erthrown by your desires,
I am friend to them and you.

[*Exit Leontes and Cleomenes.*

The history of the play during the nineteenth century begins with its revival by John Philip Kemble (1757-1823). In 1802 he presented it with splendid decorations and stage properties, the famous Mrs. Siddons, who was Kemble's sister, taking the part of Hermione. The comedy was revived again in 1856 by Charles Kean (1811-1868) at the Princess's theatre, where Ellen Terry, then a little girl, made her first appearance on the stage as Mamillius. Helen Faucit (1817-1898) about the middle of the century, and Mary Anderson (1859——) toward its close, gave brilliant interpretations of the leading female rôles. In 1910 in New York *The Winter's Tale* was admirably produced under the direction of Mr. Louis Calvert 'with such a stage and accessories as, according to the latest researches, Shakespeare had at his own command.' The most important presentation since then has been the one given by Mr. Granville Barker.

APPENDIX C

THE TEXT OF THE PRESENT EDITION

The text of the present volume is, by permission of the Oxford University Press, that of the *Oxford Shakespeare,* edited by the late W. J. Craig, except for the following deviations:

1. The stage directions and the list of *dramatis personæ* are those of the First Folio, any alterations and additions being enclosed in square brackets. The Folio numbering of scenes in the fourth act has been followed.

2. A few minor changes in punctuation (such as *good now,* for *good now* in V. i. 19) and in spelling (such as *primroses* for *prime-roses* in IV. iv. 122) have been made.

3. The following alterations, all reversions to the readings of the First Folio, have been made in the text, the reading of the Folio and the present text preceding the colon, and that of Craig following it:

I. ii. 70	nor dreamed: no nor dreamed
I. ii. 149	*Leon.* What cheer?: *Pol.* What cheer?
I. ii. 264	free of. But: free of: but
II. iii. 161	this: thy
II. iii. 177	it: its
II. iii. 189	does: doth
III. ii. 177	What flaying? boiling: What flaying? or what boiling
III. ii. 244	To: Unto
III. iii. 59	ten: sixteen
IV. iv. 594	our: her

APPENDIX D

Suggestions for Collateral Reading

William Hazlitt in *Characters of Shakespeare's Plays* (1817). (Everyman's Library edition, pp. 213-219.)

Mrs. Anna Jameson in *Characteristics of Women, Moral, Poetical and Historical* (1833).

Mary Cowden Clarke: 'Hermione; The Russian Princess' in *The Girlhood of Shakespeare's Heroines* (1850-1852). (Everyman's Library edition, vol. iii.)

A. C. Swinburne in *A Study of Shakespeare* (1880).

Helena Faucit, Lady Martin: *On Some of Shakespeare's Female Characters,* Letter no. ix. 'Hermione' (1890).

Andrew Lang: *The Comedies of Shakespeare.* With illustrations by E. A. Abbey, and comment by Andrew Lang. XII. *The Winter's Tale.* Harper's Magazine, April, 1894, vol. lxxxviii, pp. 710-720.

Barrett Wendell in *William Shakespeare* (1894).

H. H. Furness: *A New Variorum Edition of Shakespeare.* Vol. xi, *The Winter's Tale* (1898).

L. A. Sherman in *What is Shakespeare?* (1902).

Brander Matthews in *Shakspere as a Playwright* (1913).

INDEX OF WORDS GLOSSED

(Figures in full-faced type refer to page-numbers)

WITHDRAWN
LIBRARY
OF
MOUNT ST. MARY'S
COLLEGE
EMMITSBURG, MARYLAND